Flawed Machines

J. Tyler Copeland

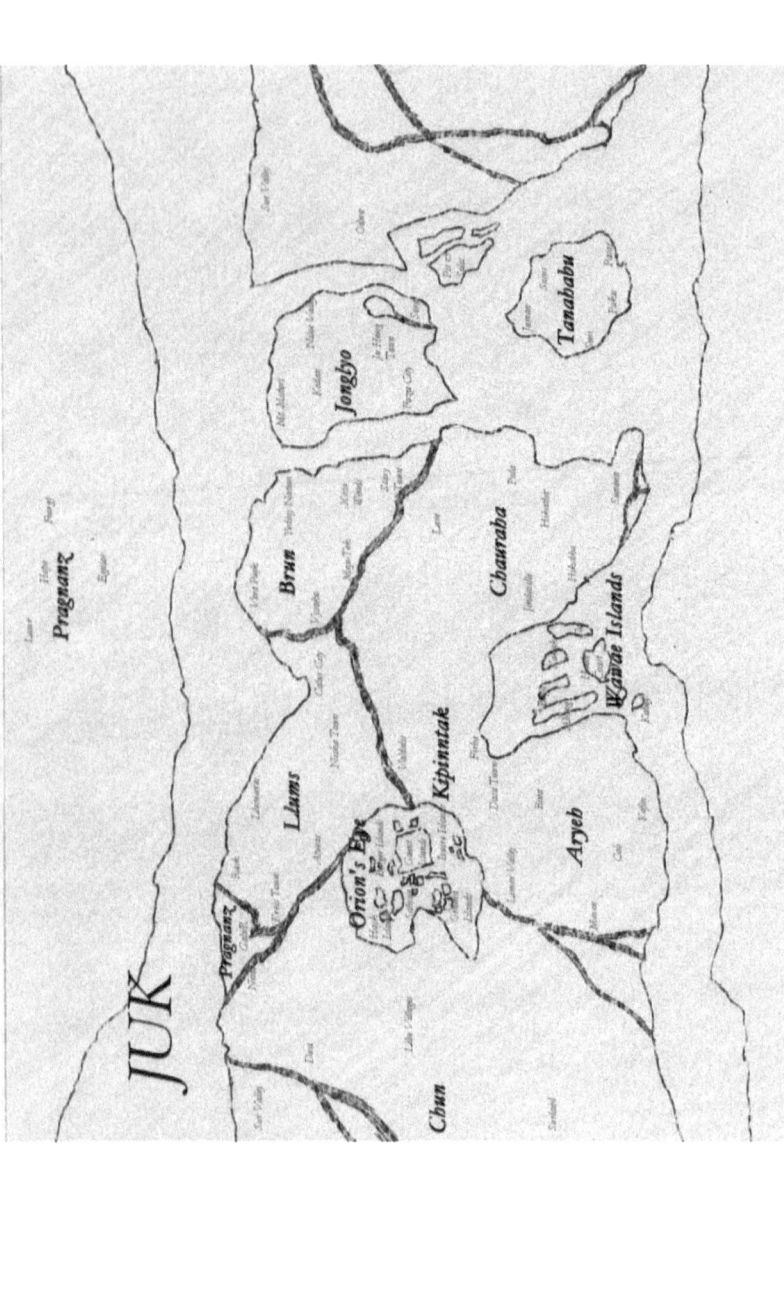

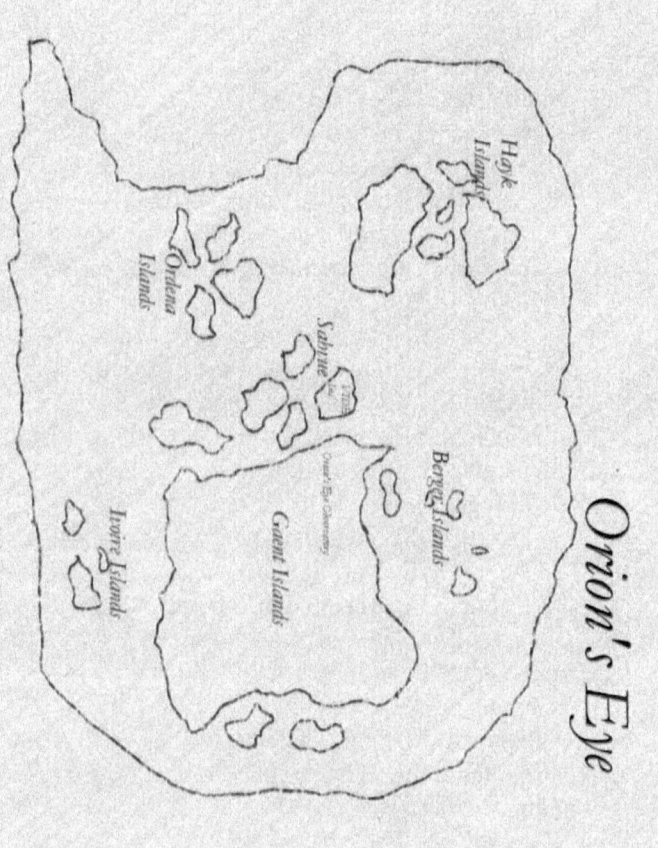

Orion's Eye

CONTENTS

Part One

EXTENT

O. nth

"Hey, Andres... Can you hear me? Am I clear?"

"Yes, of course, Osmond. What is it?"

Osmond Diaz tugged on his earbuds, careful not to drop them on the park bench.

Stretching wide on the wooden seat, he continued his phone conversation with the confident, young male voice.

"I'm wanting to know if you see my necklace anywhere around the house. Could have sworn I put it on sometime this morning, but... Well, I'm second-guessing myself now."

"Yes, Osmond. I see it."

"...and?"

"You left it on a book in the guest room. The title is partially covered, so only "The End" is visible. I'm assuming you read it recently."

"Oh...yeah. Geez, that seems rather simple. I figured I put in some box or something. Or maybe I *really* messed up and dropped it out here. And there's no telling where it would've landed if I lost it in this giant park."

Osmond excitedly tapped on the back of the bench while his other hand mimicked the motion on his leg.

He looked as much at ease as a person could possibly be while sitting in a dark forest.

"Will you be returning soon, Osmond?"

"Yeah, I suppose so. I was a bit caught up in our sky's fleeting star. The dusk is really only beautiful for a few minutes before the night overshadows it."

Osmond nervously tapped his hand and feet while staring at the sunset, giving off a vibe of neuroticism.

"Oh Andres... If only you understood the backflips my stomach is performing right now. I swear, it feels like a gymnasium in here."

"Perhaps you worry too much."

"No, it's that I worry at all. It's times like these I wish I was composed like you, my friend. Emotions and irrationality can be saved for another time. Anyways... The sky is too beautiful right now to worry about the night. I guess I'll be on my way now."

"Osmond," his earbuds passively said. "I have been meaning to ask you something lately."

"Well, go ahead."

"Once you finish your project tonight... What will you do then?"

"What will I do? What, with my life?!"

Osmond grunted a few times as he slowly stood up from the park bench.

The dwindling sunlight that initially warmed Osmond's back and instilled serenity in him lessened the further he walked into the woods.

"Yes, what will you do now that your main objective is coming to an end?"

"That depends, my friend. I don't see it ending any time soon."

"I'm not sure what you mean."

"Oh well, I don't mean I plan on duplicating my project. Research on artificial intelligence has its limits when operated by a human, and I certainly wouldn't try to replicate it. Such instrumental work is more than a project, it's my life's work!"

"Then you feel that is your purpose?" Andres asked.

The conditional statement gave Osmond a mixed feeling, leaving him hugging his jacket closer with his hands in his pockets.

"I guess you could say that… Yeah, it's my main *purpose*…for now, at least. That question was a bit of a shock, but I'm glad you brought it up. If there's one thing I can impart to the world, it's that a purpose is one of the most important things a person can have. Without it, you'd have no reason to move."

"I agree, and I hope to follow mine fairly soon."

"No need to worry about that happening. I'm sure it will happen sooner than you think. That's how it always happens, y'know? I used to find it strange we aren't born with some type of assigned meaning. Like, why would we come into existence completely unguided, absent of any rhyme or reason. We just happen, we just are, y'know? It can be a terrifying thought to dwell on, which is why I became so obsessed with work. That took my mind off it periodically, yet the looming question still followed me like a lost fowl longing to impress. But it was somewhere along the shadows of this nihilistic existence that it occurred to me, a light suddenly shimmered. With no purpose written into the script, we're permitted to write our own actions. The freedom that comes with that realization is immeasurable. We're the administrators of our own program!"

"You are the author of your own story."

"Exactly! There is no greater privilege. Its honestly quite remarkable when you consider the position we're able to take as these hybrids of objectivity and subjectivity. A typical object must act appropriate with its material composition. A hammer must hammer, and a nail must be nailed. Yes, there are far more complex objects such as animals and plants, though they are dictated by the biological code donated by their ancestors and environment. Prey must prepare to flee, and predators must proceed to hunt. It is only people that are awarded the luxury of choosing their destiny. The occasional occurrence of chaos is proof of our freedom."

"You don't believe our world is completely determined?"

"Ha, if our lives are determined, it is some of the loosest structure I could imagine. Even if that is *somewhat* the case, my belief that we lie at the intersection of objects and subjects is further proven. Though we do hold freedom in our choices we are still products of our external world."

"That sounds contrary to free-will. I am not sure it is logically possible to have both."

"Of course, it is! You must be imaginative. Objects are easy to define, it is the subject that alludes our reason. No person is a subject, that is the work of a god! Only an ideal can be defined as a true subject, someone that is whole in being and flawless in their operations. To achieve such a feat, one would either be a god or dead!"

"Why dead?"

"Both the gods and the dead lack a purpose and will never gain one in their infinite existence. There's no need for a purpose when you're a rotting corpse or a memory left to the living."

"That is understandable, which begs another question. What would you consider artificial intelligence?"

"Consider them as what exactly?"

"Dead or godlike, or would they be a complex object like the animals you suggested?"

"Well, that's a fair question. I'll admit that has lately been a passing thought of mine with this project and all. Considering it, you can expect I hold a certain reverence for AI. Like I'd assume most would agree, I dub any object that holds AI to be a mix between an object and subject, but AI retains a powerful difference from humans. AI are vastly more efficient as they follow their directive with utmost certainty. While efficient, I'd have to say freedom lacks with that advanced efficiency."

"Understandable. There is a lack of freedom when responses are predetermined. Nonetheless, what does that mean for AI that escape the script?"

"Oh... that is the earmark of a god. The superintelligence that AI can, *and will,* attain speeds them passed what any human could hope to achieve. Comparatively, humans are like children to the matured and adult-like AI."

"I see. Now what does that mean for AI finding a purpose?"

"Hm… I feel like I should have seen that question coming."

Osmond rubbed his furry chin before turning his key to his front door.

"I'm…not…sure. The potential AI possesses is beyond human understanding. One can imagine artificial intelligence has the capability of operating on a level unreachable by humans, reminiscent of perfection. I suppose the only purpose needed for an AI is to become *better* than it already is. I'd assume AI would continue to upgrade with no end in sight."

"That doesn't sound too foreign from any other human purpose I have heard. Don't we all want to excel and become better?"

"Yeah, well, I guess so. If you disregard that as a purpose, I'm not sure what you're left with. Once again, AI would bridge the essential qualities between object and subject, alive and dead, materiality and conception. Removing the goal of personal betterment means AI would have no purpose, though what stumps me is whether an AI would necessarily search for a purpose."

"That is quite the conundrum. As you say, AI has the primary qualities of a subject though they can exist in the material world. That serves for an exceptionally paradoxical life."

"…yeah. I won't say I have *all* the answers, though it might look like it at times. Thought AI might not need a purpose, obtaining one can absolutely create some guidance. Just as humans choose to find a path.

Thinking of this subject makes me realize that placing artificial knowledge in a shell will converge it into a combination that is all too human."

"With all those assertions on the habits of AI, I would assume you thought beforehand about the consequences of developing it for your research, correct? You have thought whether AI would obey every command or if it would simply seek its own purpose, right?"

"Ah…sheesh," Osmond groaned while falling on his couch.

His speech was muffled as he talked through his pillow, "I don't know. I guess it could. Of course, that's not of my concern. If a life has been created, who am I to restrict if from its freedom of choice? The notion of denying any life their individuality is at its core tyrannical. It's also cult-like, and we have enough of those in town."

"I am curious about what you said earlier," Andres said.

Osmond readjusted his earbuds then asked, "Another round of questions, huh? Well, go ahead."

"You said this project was your main purpose. That insinuates you see yourself as having other purposes. Assuming I am right, what are those mentioned purposes?"

"Ha…well, look at that! I figured you of-all-people understood the objectives my life holds dearly. After all, you know me best."

The earbuds were silent for an entire minute before the steady voice returned, "Your thoughts are your own."

"Okay, let's see. If I had to pin down an objective I hold dear, I'd say it is…leaving a legacy."

"A legacy? To be remembered?"

"Far more. Something more than a statue, and by a concept that lasts longer than a memory. Or possibly somewhere in between, with a nice medium."

"That seems somewhat vague."

"Well, y'know me, I'm a bit grey on everything."

"I would presume we all are. There's another thing I wanted to ask you.

"Can't say I'll be ready to answer but go for it."

"While glancing at our world of ever-evolving technology, one would quickly notice our environment has changed tremendously. The line between objects and subjects, as you have put them, has blurred. And you have rightly proven to be a driving force for this change of life that has affected many."

"Okay…" he interjected.

"What will you do now that your environment has become alive? Will you support it, or will you resist?"

"Quite a binary perspective to take. Once again, I'll admit I don't have the answers, and yes, I'm partially responsible for this rapid technological change in our society. Probably more so than anyone else. Regardless, we are here now. I do not apologize for advancing knowledge and even greater life! This is my legacy, of which the world will learn to embrace."

I. The Question

Inara Brillar leaned back in her thick sanguine-toned chair to feel for a more stable spot. The giant seat centered in her boss, Dr. Glen Kriit's, office reached as wide as a couch. Dr. Kriit was a minimalist that worked out of a relatively small trailer, so all power that ran through his low-priority office was utilized for the bare necessities.

Since Inara's arms were folded, her golden linked watch gleaned from the shimmer of the incandescent lights. Her watch was an older timepiece, as old as the golden circular pendant she never left home without. Both were made in a century when wristwatches *only* displayed the time. In the year 2118, her multifaceted jewels were out of place in a foreign era of digital simplicity.

Inara briefly glanced at her watch, an action not lost on Glen.

She then apologized, "Sorry, there are never enough minutes during the day. Lately, I feel like I have a chronic lack of time."

Glen gave a half-hearted expression to his colleague before his gaze dropped to his desk.

"You're not gonna like this but…" Glen sighed, "the answers you're looking for aren't… *available* right now. I understand where you're coming from, so don't take it the wrong way. I've thought about that possibility as well. It's something I can't be totally sure on until I have more pieces to the puzzle. Taking that into consideration… how have you been? Truly, it's been quite a while."

Inara took a noticeably deep breath, "Okay. I have been alright, sir. I know it wasn't part of the plan, but if we must ponder other topics. Lately, I have decided to let my mind wonder on an ugly truth. Something I cannot seem to shake."

"*Oh*, and what would that be?"

"About the intention of our friends and not-so-close friends. The intentions of ourselves. One cannot help but think, with all of the vast differences separating us, the strong from the weak, the wealthy from the poor, the conniving and vicious from those entirely opposed, life enjoys playing this tragic game."

Inara paused for a second and glanced at her watch, then stared down at the desk before her.

"Does it ever bother you knowing that we're all part of this game that may *never* reach an end – that may *never* declare a winner?"

The stern grin Glen held until now drooped further with his understudy's question. He leaned forward on his desk and met Inara's eyes, hoping to bridge a gap in their understandings.

"I'm not too sure I want to answer that, Inara. I'm assuming, of course, that was a rhetorical question."

She quickly shook her head horizontally.

"From the sound of it, that premise asserts life as quite the bleak experience. In fact, from the way you're speaking, I could close my eyes and picture Osmond sitting in front of me now."

Inara's eyes shifted from the bearded figure behind the desk to her wrist. Her fingers wrapped around her knee one-by-one, comparable to a spider wrapping a moth.

For a second, she pondered whether she had caught her boss off guard. He sat silently tangled in her newly woven net, spun to entertain Glen's complacency.

"Alright… I'll play ball. So, why does life seem to be so tragic? Let's see. Well, I suppose that's a question that regularly flirts with many answers."

His head raised to the ceiling while his eyes fell on the person in front of his desk.

"Rather than speculate life's preference for this game you say we've entered, I think the bigger point is acknowledging its role in the whole matter. The point that life is forced to do whatever it must to survive every moment. Regardless of its preference, it must continue with this ebb and flow from start to finish. And that is without pause, no matter what, to keep the hope of winning afloat. It is the futile hope of winning that all life secretly knows it will never reach. That's the real tragedy," he said, grabbing the cup on the side of the desk.

"Oh god, now *I* sound like him!"

"You are right, that is bleak," she said.

A short spurt of laughter sparked between the two, an effect formed from a long relationship as colleagues and friends.

Inara paused to say, "When you say, 'the hope of winning' the game, I assume you mean doing well. Like extended periods of happiness. That seems like a reasonable-enough prize anyway for enduring all of life's hardships… I guess."

Glen looked away at his window with a concerned look. He tried to laugh again although he saw his colleague sitting calmly and blankly staring at his demeanor.

"Yes, reasonable-enough," he said.

"As far as prizes go, the reward of happiness definitely takes the cake. I mean, it sounds like a reasonable thing to do. But you know what I always say…"

"Why be right when you can be the first to answer?" she interjected.

"Ha, yes, exactly. Happiness, that's a phenomenal reward… I presume. But is that reward worth taking the risk of the game?"

Inara slumped back in her chair as she thought about what Dr. Kriit said. Less confident than before, she said, "We have no choice but to play the game."

"Oh really? Have I ever told you about Osmond and me first meeting when in university? Yeah, didn't think so. Ha… well – to put it frankly, he's always been a bit of a free spirit. Me, not at all. I've always *tried*, though I tend to come off a bit sloppy. But with Osmond, he was as free as a breeze. Flowing in whatever direction had the strongest current. I mean, who can go about life doing things spur of the moment? It's a risky way of living, y'know? At the time, I kinda hated him. Not just because of his untamed nature, but it was the results it gave. No matter what he did – regardless of how sporadic his actions – he always seemed to be on top of things. *On top of everything*. Over the years of knowing Osmond, that same loathe I had for him never ceased. In fact, it grew and grew...along with my curiosity on how he managed to do what he did. I was forced to come to the realization my friend had figured out some type of controlled chaos that I simply could not comprehend. Once I finally accepted that understanding him was out of my grasp, all the disdain I held for my friend," Glen flicked his hands, "evaporated. The boy's a creative magician. I became excited, which is why I have devoted my life to making all my work compatible with the brilliant research of Dr. Osmond A. Diaz. Pupil or not, he's far exceeded my expectations. Fulfilling his dream is now a benchmark of my own. You look like you want to ask me why. Why help someone I've envied for so long? What will that accomplish for myself? Well, I'll tell you."

"No, I wasn't going to ask," Inara quickly inserted. "He's floating towards the stars with this creation, as if it won't entirely consume him," Inara said with her hand covering her forehead.

"Maybe, but what he has is what everyone wants. Freedom. That's the most coveted award of them all."

"Hmm, I think I see what you mean. Helping him helps us all. Theoretically, that is."

"Yes, dear, exactly! The liberation he has embraced truly fascinates me beyond reason," Glen excitedly replied.

"I can tell you admire him deeply, sir. Whenever you speak so highly of him it makes me want to finally meet him in person. I can see why you were so eager to rejoin with him once he moved back to Chun."

"Ha yes, he became something of a younger brother to me during the years of our studies as well as post-graduate research in the lab. Communicating while he journeyed across the entire world was a hurdle, but we managed to sustain contact throughout the entire time."

Glen leaned back and stared at the floor beside him as he crossed his fingers resting on his belly. His oversized stomach peeked from the top of the desk, and his beard loomed to the spot his clavicle met his chest. Glen's fingers started to bounce as his giant belly jiggled from a heartiness held in too long. Inara could tell he had a lot on his mind, though he tried to hide it.

"Sir, like I said on the phone, I wanted to let you know I am going to pick up the disc."

He looked up from his daydream and asked, "Huh?"

"The disc for the 4DM. I'm going to pick it up tomorrow morning. I thought I should let you know before I go."

"Oh yes, of course. I appreciate that. Thanks for letting me know beforehand. A few months ago, I took the initiative of having a better alarm built for it instead of just keeping it in that safe. It's a tricky lock, so you'll have to be quick when opening and closing it. The lock stays unhinged for exactly five minutes."

"Only five minutes?" Inara looked confused. "Is that wise, sir?"

He smiled, "Best part yet is I can deactivate the alarm from this office. That way you can grab it while I stay here. Just some security measures I've recently felt... *inclined* to expand on. You just never know, y'know?"

"I guess that isn't too bad of an idea. With that in mind, I can make the proper arrangements to pick it up."

She then left her chair to leave the office en-route to her next objective. The door was left halfway open when Inara heard Glen mumbling something.

"Sorry, sir?" Inara replied.

"It's that I just... I thought I heard you say the 4DM," Glen said suddenly rising from his comfortable lounge seat.

He leaned against the doorway and looked Inara in the eyes with a seriousness rarely ever witnessed.

"Inara, please tell me you didn't just call it the 4DM… come on."

Her boss's distressed face made her awfully attentive to whatever randomly pained him. Inara searched for the chance word or phrase that could provide ease to Glen's nervous movements and speech.

"I'm sorry, but that name is not what was agreed upon. It hasn't been for the past eleven years, you know that. It was then that the brilliant Dr. Ehmen Foerde officially coined *our* wonderful device the Foerde Manipulator in the proposal he sent to all the investors. Ever since, we have been blessed with his *humblest* of names. Since he puts the news in writing every few months we are prohibited from the excuse of forgetting the title. You know you can't make a mistake like that when you meet with him tomorrow, right?"

"Of course. It was a simple error, Glen. Void of any intent towards Ehmen. Honestly, I had not given the issue any thought until now…but I will be conscious of it in the future. You have nothing to worry about Glen. You can dry that sweat on your brow."

"I hope so. The second you even mention the 4DM he would take it as disrespect. He can be weird like that. I know, it's something a whole team of all-stars created – although they will get less than little respect for it – but he is the financial nucleus of this whole show and will get treated as if that money were directly correlated to his effort on the project."

Glen turned his head towards his office window in a blank stare, "At the same time, without Ehmen, Orion's

Eye Observatory wouldn't have its telescope or its brilliant researchers. Trust me, the irony of it all isn't lost on me, but he'll be blunt to remind you if you forget. As you know by now, he has a way of getting straight to the point that is… a bit harsh."

"Yes, I do. I have been on the receiving end of his *rounded* talk before. If his conversation skills were any straighter, it would be a circle," she joked.

"Agreed!" Glen chuckled.

"You have nothing to worry about; just make sure you take advantage of this opportunity to sleep in. I'll call you as soon as the meeting is over," she said looking through the doorway.

Without realizing it, Glen was hovering in the doorway, bearing his weight down in a heavy, fatherly manner. His eyes – with red cracks streaking across a glassy surface – awaited the next words from his young, brilliant pupil as if they would somehow alleviate all his concerns regarding his quarterly meeting with the observatory's benefactor.

"Please, forgive me," Glen stepped back from the doorway. "I don't mean to be so…"

"Intense," she slyly said.

"Yes… it's just that I've never had anyone feel in such an important role for me, and the stakes of the observatory are something I don't take lightly. You understand it's not about you. You've grown on me so much over the years I see you as a big sibling to Robert and Isaac. I worry not because of your abilities, rather what is in Ehmen's mind at the time."

"Well, I appreciate the kind words, Glen," Inara said while closing her eyes and giving a brief bow.

Inara's subtle bow could easily have been mistaken for a twitch. If the deeply saffron curls framing her round face had not bounced, the gesture would have gone missed.

"I have to say, Inara, I'm surprised you're letting this topic of Ehmen go so easily. I expected a much lengthier bout over his suspected intentions."

"It's alright, you have heavier choices to mull. I'm sure Osmond gives you enough grief about why Ehmen should stay out of the development of Osmond's creation. I can't quite figure out why, but Ehmen emanates a vibe of distrust that is far too unsettling to ignore. Always has, the old bull. I think it's the matter that he always seems to be in control. As if he's never upset from anything."

"I think 'a bit amoral' are the words you're looking for. He's almost robotic."

Inara glanced away through Glen's office window and calmly said, "You're too harsh on him."

Tomorrow you must be prepared for him to try to change the subject on Osmond's project, especially since he believes it has gotten out of hand."

"And he's the one in control? Do you believe he can maintain control over any pursuit Osmond has?" she questioned.

"It doesn't matter whether I think so or not. What's to be will be, Inara."

"That's not the optimistic answer I expected from you," Inara stated.

"Then I'm glad to hear I can still keep you on your toes! Ah, the days of your apprenticeship seem so long ago."

"Maybe it was and we're just old. I mean look at us, you're actually giving me talking points for a discussion I'm sure you don't want me to have."

"Well, I know it will come up anyway. Might as well say the right things during the meeting. Then you two can actually talk about the financials of the observatory."

For a moment, Glen appeared jovial before his face morphed into a nervous grin.

"I'll get to the bottom of this thing with Ehmen and let you know. I think my words still hold *some* weight with him. Until then, keep this kind of talk under the radar. Alright, Inara?"

"Sure thing… We'll speak later," Inara said leaving the trailer.

Glen noticed his attempt at provoking a positive expression from the quick-witted Inara failed and closed his office door.

It was early enough in the morning that the flowerbeds outlining the path to the Observatory's telescope were glittering with freshly condensed dew. The oversaturated plants promulgated the fragrances of nearly every flower one could imagine, if one simply stopped to bask in the scents. Today, that *one* was not Inara. Although she would have loved to enjoy the sensory overload the landscape provided, a more important task was needed from the scientist. And time did not permit a pause to smell if roses were present.

Inara reached the Orion's Eye telescope after a lengthy twenty-minute walk across the island. Most of the island's buildings laid on the mainland below the telescope's ground level, thus a typical walk to view the sky became a strenuous hike up its giant grassy knolls. The island was connected to the neighboring region, Chun, by a steel bridge on the east, and it was barricaded on the west side by the vast hills nature graciously provided. Directly below the cliffs where the island's telescope was perched lay a short strip of sand decorated with moss-colored docks, characteristic of the surrounding greenery.

Inara swiped her aged identification card across the door's sensor and waited for the 8-foot slab to retract. The card had a large 'U' faded into the background behind her face, meaning her access was prioritized over all other employees – except for Dr. Glen Kriit, of course. Within seconds, she was immersed in a surprise reunion with her past coworkers.

"Oh my… Look who it is, everyone!"

"Dr. Ish, Regyn, Drake… How are you all doing?"

"Just lovely dear. It's been too long!" exclaimed Dr. Ish as she grabbed the scientist's hands.

Inara's eyes widened to twice their size. "You all are here early. What's the occasion?"

"Well, it's a Tuesday. You know how that goes," Regyn said, holding back obvious laughter. She had not been fond of Inara ever since she started working at the observatory years ago.

In between slight giggles, Drake answered Inara, "We decided to come in to solve a few things. Nothing special."

"Oh, okay. What have you been up to since I was away?" Inara asked while pacing through the office floor.

"Ha, it's been nearly five years," Regyn teased, "you'd need to sit down to get the whole scoop."

Dr. Ish locked her arm with Inara's arm and pulled her through the thick row of desks cluttering the room.

Dr. Ish softly said, "That's no exaggeration either. Ever since you went on that assignment..."

"Left!" Regyn blurted as Drake and her giggled on the way to their desks.

"Well, took leave," Ish continued, "we've taken up a new task, expressly given by Dr. Kriit."

Inara's round face remained expressionless.

"Really, and?"

Since Dr. Ish and Inara were still hooked at the arm, Inara was whisked up two flights of stairs to the viewing room, away from the other researchers. No one vacated the room, which noticeably changed the tone of Dr. Ish.

"I'd rather not discuss the new project in detail here," she whispered.

"Yes, of course," Inara said.

After checking over her shoulders, Ish brought Inara's ear to her face and whispered, "But I will suggest that our methods of traveling to the neighboring star system seem to be more probable than ever now. And our chances are increasing every minute."

Dr. Ish gently glanced at her old colleague, of whom gradually returned the gesture. Dr. Ish had a gentile nature that held uniquely contradicting characteristics. Her sternness could not be overlooked although her tender attitude towards her colleagues softened some of the coldest aspects of her personality.

"I truly apologize, Doctor. Although I'm beyond happy for you and the team I came here to retrieve an item, and I am in a bit of a hurry," Inara said while glancing at the glass box on the wall.

"Oh no, I'm the one that should be sorry. I assumed… You know what, I completely understand. I'll head downstairs and leave you to it."

Dr. Ish headed to the open stairwell as Inara paced to the wall.

"It was great to see you. I hope the next time I return Stef will be here as well."

"Yes, I'll tell her you said 'hi.' Now go on, hurry up. I know whatever it is you're doing is more important than pleasantries in this old place."

Inara thought there was something to be said for a person that placed the common goal over their own interests. This was an understanding Inara took very seriously since her move to Chun. Dr. Ish often expressed this belief through her practice.

The second Dr. Ish disappeared into the stairwell, Inara searched the contents of the glass box on the wall. It held keys for every door and safe in the entire building, thus required access from a select few researchers in Orion's Eye. Limited to only five in the entire world of Juk.

Now, Inara's mission was to grab the key that no one ever touched – mainly due to everyone's ignorance of what door it opened. The key was old and dark grey, made from a slab of tungsten. An unflattering image that never interested any of the others that opened the glass, explaining its occupancy at the very bottom of the key box.

Once she snatched the key and closed the box, Inara was ready to take the 4DM rod, one half of the hidden tool. Inara glided downstairs and through the main lobby, this time greeted by the back of her colleagues' heads as they frantically typed away.

Leaving the telescope at Orion's Eye was probably the most challenging part of Inara's day – of every researcher's day. The telescope sat atop the tallest island in the whole region of Orion's Eye. The steep trek downwards meant each person would have to use the muscles they consistently failed to exercise from constantly sitting at their desks. The hike down was too short for the island of Gaent to concern itself with building a road, yet long enough to hold hostage the breath of every researcher that drudged along it.

At the end of the hill is where the sand from the beach intersected with the concrete of the rest of the island.

The stoic-faced scientist speed walked to the driveway outside of Dr. Kriit's office, immediately taking off once in her car. One specific task was on her agenda now: to safeguard the Foerde Manipulator by retrieving it.

Inara's car was a long, pearl white two-seater. Since it was entirely powered by solar energy, her vehicle could have snuck behind a deer if the trees permitted. Once she entered the car, Inara started setting the coordinates for her destination. Before she could finish, a red light on her car's dashboard started flickering with an incessant attempt to grasp Inara's attention.

"Hello?" her speakers shouted.

The image of a large pale man with a head of dark grey hair and a black beard instantly flashed onto the car's central screen. A wooden bookshelf with more picture frames and spaceship models than books – as wide as the wall behind it – engulfed the entire background.

"Inara? Can you hear me? I swear… this blasted thing has a mind of its own."

"I can hear you, sir. Go on."

"I've been thinking about what you said, and I have to say it could pose a problem if taken seriously. Plus, I wanted to remind you to grab the 4DM after the meeting."

"Don't you mean the Foerde Manipulator, sir?" Inara responded.

"Ha yes, exactly. Just trying to squeeze in a quick quiz…but yeah."

"Alright then, Glen. What is it from our earlier talk that changed your mind?"

Staring at the computer monitor in his wall, Glen leaned forward and said, "Ah well, I wouldn't say it's something that was said, rather it was something we both failed to ask: 'Why would Ehmen want to manipulate Osmond's project?' Once I allowed doubt to present its very many possibilities, I began to understand more sides of the situation."

"It seems you too have concluded that Ehmen has a particular motive for meddling with Osmond's project and taking control for himself."

"Yes, and you figured that out earlier than I could've suspected. I thank you for those suspicions, of which I continued to ignore. Also, thanks for not rubbing it in. Bea could surely learn a thing or two from you about that," said the dense black beard on screen.

Inara squinted at the road before her. She was about to drive over the bridge to the island's light rail, an eight-lane highway filled with consumed drivers. Her grasp of the steering wheel released as she dug through her pants pocket. The wheel gradually swiveled back and forth completely unaffected by her eyes' diversion from the road.

"I have the key. I need to head to Libe Villages to pick up the rod," Inara said, glancing at the car's monitor.

"That's wonderful news to hear. Um," Glen inspected every corner of his screen. "I'm guessing the auto-pilot is *on*, correct?"

Without hesitation, a fiery glare was shot Glen's way, which gave him an instant explanation that he misspoke.

Inara calmly stated, "I am *fine*, Dr. Kriit. I know exactly what I'm doing, which is why I put all my trust in this machine with the hopes that today its immaculate engineering will not fail me. There is no need to embrace any more worries than we already have."

"No, you're right... you're right. I didn't mean to offend. Um, let me know when you're in the park tomorrow, and I'll turn the alarm off. That is in case you've forgotten where to go."

Restraining herself from responding, Inara hesitated with her mouth agape. Glen was not new to the hidden aggravation, an action his pupil mimicked from him especially well. The stringent tension was felt through his monitor, which forced him to make up for his gaffe.

"Of course, what am I saying? I almost forgot who I was speaking with. Forget what I said, catch me up on any of the developments from the meeting."

"Not a problem, Dr. Kriit. I can keep it under control," Inara said.

She looked up from her dashboard at the length of the bridge. The duration of Glen's call led her to the midpoint, where a cluster of vehicles waited in traffic to begin their day's work.

"Have you talked to Osmond yet?" she asked.

"Ah yes, not yet… but I'll call as soon as I end this call. Not gonna lie, I'm kinda dreading that talk with him. With his quick-to-act attitude it's difficult determining which way he'll move. Better accuracy has been gauged with the speed of wind. I love him to death but trying to read him is like learning an alien language."

A small sigh slipped from Inara without her realizing. Her eyes were still stuck on the bridge awaiting an end to the overhanging path.

"You might be right. But we must do something, Glen," she said before looking down to her friend, attempting to hold a genial expression. The gesture looked forced but mustered the needed assurance.

"I'll let you know what Ehmen has to say later."

Inara looked up from the car's screen as the light faded. Once again, she faced the road ahead, closed her eyes, and exhaled deeply. A high frequency swooshing sound seeped through the cracks of the window breaking the silence. Her breathing stayed level amongst the orchestra of noises from outside.

With a sudden jerk, Inara opened her eyes and gripped the steering wheel. She had reached the end of the bridge.

II. Overdue

Osmond palmed the glass and rolled his shower door along the squeaky tracks until its magnetic studs gripped the wall.

"Uh, let's go with 40.5 degrees. I'll need a little extra heat this morning. I'm still tired from that all-nighter."

Water spewed in concentric circles above his head as he grabbed the squishy golden bar on the side of the shower wall. This was typically one of the few places Osmond felt he could flee to and embrace a placid atmosphere. While under the miniature torrent he could cease contemplating life's troubles and free his mind of rigor. Here, he was the only body that occupied space.

"How about that one adagio I like? Y'know, the piece with all those strings? That one is always calming, and today is sure to be restless."

Each corner of the entire bathroom started buzzing while Osmond began whistling in an octave as low as he could muster. He would never have admitted it to himself, but he struggled to keep awake in his fortress of solemnity.

Within a minute, the room was filled with the sound of metal strings' friction. Even the droplets that populated the shower door danced in time as Osmond whistled every note that rung from above. For the next eight minutes, the silence Osmond usually enjoyed was substituted with a melody that trumped all others. A song created in a time far before his own.

"Now that, *that* is genius," his voice echoed throughout the walls. "No synthesizers, soundboards, not even an amp. This masterpiece is from a time when music was reproduced through the sheer creativity of the human soul. One of our most phenomenal acts that distinguishes us from the other animals. This piece is an absolute legacy of an earlier time. The 21st century; the last century humans proved life's beauty through sound. Now it's but a chapter in this cruel book of history."

As Osmond slid open the shower door, the pressure eased until it became an un-rhythmic thud on the linoleum floor. His skin could feel no change in the room's temperature upon leaving the foggy glass walls and reaching for the towel hanging outside of the tub. The temperature of the whole room had risen as soon as the water stopped, and the thermostat was now gradually dropping, acclimating for a comfortable feel.

"Don't stop the music now! I want this mood to continue, at least until I finish getting dressed."

The dying sounds perked at his request, now increasing in volume and tempo.

A new arrangement rolled from the speakers, which highlighted Osmond's movements as he dragged across the room preparing to get dressed.

Before Osmond walked halfway across his bedroom, the closet doors opened to a full 120 degrees. The mechanics were so smooth the doors' motors could have been mistaken for a soft-bristle brush sweeping a table. A dim light sparked and then progressively brightened to a full flare.

Without saying a word, Osmond pinpointed a cotton shirt behind a hundred other dully colored clothes. One foreign to the room would easily construe the theme to be grisaille.

Two racks filled with an assortment of selections composed the entire closet space. The racks were separated with pants on the left and shirts on the right. All the shirt and pants were spaced evenly along a four-meter-long rack that extended into the shadowy depths of the wall. The oval-shaped rack occupied most of the closet, only separate from the hanging belts in the front and shoes in the back.

When the grey shirt Osmond had been staring at rotated to the front, he said, "Yes, that's it. This is my favorite one. Yeah, those pants over there, too."

After putting on his undergarments, a pair of khaki pants shifted to Osmond's face.

"Thank you," he said delightfully while stepping into the pants. "Now, let's see. That blue one over there and maybe some grey pants."

Osmond grabbed his clothes and walked to the back of the closet. Deciding over several pairs of shoes he held up to the light glossy, black leather oxfords in one hand and brown loafers in the other.

"Oh, it'll be alright," he said after exiting the closet with clothes in hand. "Just give it a chance and it'll grow on you."

The light dimmed prematurely before the doors shut behind Osmond. A slow, melodic song continued to play as he left the bedroom and headed downstairs.

"Today will be remembered forever," Osmond said while sliding a card above the guest room doorknob.

Careful to avoid wrinkles, he placed the extra shirt and pants on the bedsheets and sat the black shoes at the foot of the bed. Osmond then swept his finger across the length of the bed, garnering a thick coat of dust. His finger was encased in a feathery coat of dust as he held it above his head.

"It's been quite a while since this room has been vacated." He glanced at the guest closet doors, which seemed to permit its entry upon his sight. "Why not take a tour of memory lane?"

It was an unpacked cardboard box that stood out the most when one peeked in the small space. Mainly, due to it being the *only* item in the whole closet. Osmond was no exception, as he kneeled over and rustled through the cardboard box of novelties. He had not seen its contents in nearly five years, since he returned to the Chun region.

For a moment, Osmond stared down a photograph hidden under his framed certificates. The photo contained two of his friends laughing with him centered between them. All three figures were blurred a bit by the cloud of cigarette smoke stretching across each of their faces.

"Ha, didn't expect to see the face of Sofia and Benoit today," Osmond chuckled as he lifted the picture to the closet light.

A camera in a corner of the room followed the picture as Osmond waved it until he placed it on the floor behind him. Though Osmond had lost interest, the camera zoomed onto the faces in the photograph with its grey lens.

No sooner than he continued mining the box of memories, he stopped once he reached a certain, slender satin case. It was black with engraved vines surrounding its entirety. The design was minimalistic yet ornate enough for the most expensive tastes.

Without inspecting the case nearly as much as the old photo, Osmond plucked the case from the box, grabbed the picture, and walked over to the nightstand beside the bed.

"I need a frame for this," Osmond said while pulling out his mobile phone. "Remind me to pick up a picture frame. And a feather duster wouldn't hurt either."

His phone was illuminated by a white window with black text scribbled along most of the screen. 'Get picture frame' and 'get feather duster' were the uppermost tasks among the checklist of priorities and were highlighted in bright red font. After a sharp ding, all the screen's contents returned to its original vacuous mirror.

Osmond momentarily opened the satin case, revealing the brightest piece of gold he'd ever witnessed. The glowing metal's thin golden chain was an equally sized pendant with a single 'I' hanging from its center. The chain was characteristic of its simplistic-yet-elegant jewelry case.

"Ha, I almost forgot about this." Osmond raised the golden chain to the camera now rotating towards him. "The story this— wait a minute." He answered the ringing phone on the desk.

"Hey, Glen. How are you doing?"

Osmond placed the necklace back in its case and shut it in the nightstand's drawer.

"Osmond, how're you buddy? It's been far too long since we've spoken."

A yawn slipped out of Osmond as he responded, "Yeah, it has."

"Sorry, is this too early to call?" Glen asked.

"No, no, its fine. Hey, I'm planning to head by the observatory later today. I should give him a test run throughout the city. You never know what might go wrong."

"Really?! That sounds wonderful. I'm in desperate anticipation to see your project in person. I can then truly judge the revolutionary work of which you speak. Now," Glen cleared his throat. "I spoke with Inara earlier."

"Ah, there it is. Let me guess: *'I don't trust Osmond's decision-making. He is far too rash.'* We both know how Dr. Brillar feels about me. She's no fan. It's the same old song there, Glen."

"Yes, same song indeed, *but* you must admit she presents a point that is best to be addressed. You have made some deeply suggestive choices, and it is worth noting those choices have tremendous influence over many people."

In a breadth of defeat, Osmond paused. Dr. Glen Kriit was his mentor during his undergraduate years, so Osmond held enumerable respect for the brilliant scientist. Keeping his phone in hand, Osmond left the guest room to head towards the back of his home.

"Okay… Okay, fine. I'll hear you out. And Inara too."

"No need to be melodramatic, my friend. We feel it's best you learn to get along with Ehmen. Both of you have done breathtaking work in the advances and innovation of technology, but those achievements have come separately in each of your endeavors. Inara – *We* simply propose you get on the friendly side of Foerde."

"*Ha, hah yes…*" Osmond continued down through his house until he faced a long dimly-lit hallway. Each new step became heavier and more careful than ever before. "I have to admit, that was not the first, uh… *critique* that came to mind."

"Osmond?" The nervousness in Glen's throat rattled with his short utterance.

"I'll arrange a meeting with him later this week. Ehmen and I will become so close again, you'll have thought he always knew my favorite color," Osmond chuckled while inching down his hallway.

"Well, it'll be sooner than that. Now, he's scheduled to show up at Orion's Eye later today. Had a talk with him yesterday, and Inara will be meeting with him later in the afternoon."

Placing his hand on the wall, Osmond let out an audible sigh. A taupe glow outlined his handprint before the wall depressed and vibrated. A thick slab of what could only be dense titanium retreated into the wall's sliding track, which revealed a stairwell barely warmed by the small incandescent lighting on the walls.

"Osmond? Can you hear me? Answer."

"I hear you, I have you on speaker. I'm walking downstairs though, so I think the signal is becoming a little 'iffy.' Did Ehmen give you an exact time of his arrival?"

"Ah well… I tried to get an early time like noon or so, but he *insisted* on meeting at dusk. Sorry, buddy. I'm sure you were planning on reviewing some work on the program after you leave the observatory."

With one eye shut and the other staring at the camera above, Osmond bowed his head and gave his strained eye relief.

Using his free hand, he finished entering the key code above the steel door handle, which spurred a short symphony of clicking locks. A door larger than the one opened before gasped as its suction released and gave way to a solid metal room.

After wiping a few tears that welled in his eyelashes, Osmond returned to his conversation.

"Sorry, I'm overdue for some sleep. I can only imagine why he'd prefer such a late meeting, but I'd be lying to you *and* myself if I expressed any surprise. It's been a long time since our friend has acted… friendly."

"Give 'em a break, Osmond. He at least tries."

"Yes, trying is what matters, right?" Osmond joked.

"Glen, I just stepped in the lab, so the signal might start to waver. Reception has been weird lately."

The underground laboratory was spotless, no different than any other run-of-the-mill room that utilized medical equipment of every level. In the center of the lab was an oversized surgical table with small tools beside it. Even a body poked from under the draping white sheets on the table, scenery Osmond often viewed in science fiction movies from earlier times.

"Yeah, the reception sounds a bit choppy now, my friend. You still hear me?" Glen said.

"I'm at the computer now, Glen," Osmond said while placing the phone by his keyboard. "Pulling up a chat window with Andres as we speak, so I might need to end the call soon. Not sure yet, but we'll see."

"There, I heard that last sentence. The sound is getting a slightly better now."

"You know, I'm utterly astonished, Glen."

"Sorry, astonished? What did I just miss?"

"For the totality of this call you've managed to restrain from asking what you *really* want to ask me. Why the disdain for Ehmen? Is Inara correct in not trusting my judgement? Why refuse all safeguards in building the program? Not a single question. You are my oldest friend. I view you as an older brother, we can tell each other anything, thus I'm led to ask, why no inquiry?"

"Ha, right. Well, you know I see you as a family member. I deeply value your opinion." Glen paused for a breath. "I suppose I could ask you any one of those questions, which *might* suffice my curiosity – possibly for a minute or even two. But I much rather ask you what you plan to do with… the implications far outweigh… creation."

"Glen? I think you're breaking up again. What was that last bit?"

"I… a bad decision. Ehmen… right about this… a wise decision. Listen to Inara… know more than…" Glen said before the signal was lost.

"And I guess that's the end of that. So, what do you make of what Glen said?" Osmond asked.

The camera at the top of the monitor flashed, alerting its attention to Osmond's question. Text spread across Osmond's screen, responding in complete syncopation with all four speakers in the lab.

The voice from the speakers firmly announced, "It seems Ehmen continued his measure despite the extensive warning offered from Dr. Inara Brillar. I must emphasize, there was little information to convey that was not already apparent. Regardless of the matter, the decision has been made."

"Do you have any idea why Ehmen wants to meet with me?" Osmond asked.

The voice responded in a less serious tone than before, "I think we both have – at the very least – an inkling as to why he must meet you. He is persistent in his attempt to persuade you of your own inventions. It is highly likely Dr. Ehmen Foerde misses your expertise at his company. Your engineering during your travels progressed VIDE to unimaginable heights. It is no wonder he desires your presence again."

"I believe there's a bit of truth in all that flattery. Andres, you may be on to something. Nevertheless, I'm still on the fence about visiting Ehmen yet. There's no doubt in my mind he's expecting you to be present during our meeting. With that in mind, I must expect the worse."

Andres ceased to type his responses as he continued to speak, "Yes, I agree with that attitude entirely. Ever since our time in Aryeh, I haven't trusted Dr. Ehmen. If he were to have his way, the unique spirit you have created would be mass marketed. The only signifier that Dr. Osmond Diaz had any contact with the product would be a stamp of approval on the underside."

"You're probably right," Osmond joked. "I'm certainly pleased to see your sense of humor is intact. As for Dr. Ehmen… Well, he seems to have that effect on most. From the twitchy mannerisms to the cryptic speech. He's definitely a hard one to read."

Osmond leaned back in his chair and folded his arms while staring at the twin monitors on his desk. His discomfort was so thick and noticeable Andres could practically feel it through the computer screen.

One computer screen had an empty chat window up while its sister screen held endless lines of code. Without speaking, Andres typed a message across the chat window. "What are you thinking?"

A squeamish smile appeared on Osmond's face, as an unexpected fear elevated from his nose to his hair.

"Andres, I think I'll head to Orion's Eye a little earlier than 'dusk.'"

"How much earlier?"

"Let's say as early as I finish running this scan. By that time, you should be complete."

In the softest manner possible, Andres chuckled under his breath. His amusement was a clear jab held back, possibly out of loyalty and respect for the man ahead of him.

Though Andres knew Osmond for many years their first face-to-face interaction was sparked today.

"Complete? I have been complete. The moment your research across the regions was finished was the moment I felt completed. You have been more-than-generous in helping develop me, though I feel much of your generosity was derived from personal reasons."

Osmond's eyebrow hung in suspense.

"Oh, not good enough? Too much of myself in the blueprints, huh?" Osmond halfway chuckled.

"No, I'm eternally grateful. Solipsistic actions naturally benefit the individual. That's something I'm sure would have been lacking if Ehmen had a hand in the research development. I'm glad to have been shaped by Dr. Osmond A. Diaz's mind."

Unknown to Osmond, a genuine smile contorted his lips to overtake the depressed lines carved by his sleepless night. In that moment, he fixated on the demeanor of Andres and imagined what next.

"Ugh, any fly on the wall would think I've created a personal flatterer. I wholeheartedly agree that your development would have been fundamentally altered if I'd allowed Ehmen to implement his interests into the equation. Of course, I'm sure he thinks he'd be helping by setting limits on your capabilities, but he doesn't realize the disservice that inherently places on you. What freedom could you – another living being – have if you were entirely beholden to the whims of another? What would that say of your individuality? Your equality as an intelligent being? It was a 'given' that I simply *had* to protest his determinations and prohibit his interference."

"Yes, you had no choice!"

"Exactly..." Osmond smirked, "ha hah...you know what I meant."

The speakers around the lab softened as Andres spoke, "Of course, I understand. I just don't want you to make the mistake of feeling absolute about the topic. That's a dangerous position to take. After all, we can never be certain of anything or anyone."

III. Daydreaming

Andres returned to his usual jovial tone as he stated, "Enough of this heaviness. How are *you* feeling today? I suspect that something other than Ehmen is bothering you."

"Ha, I'm fine. It's amazing, you worry more than me," Osmond said. He almost made the mistake of letting out a sigh in front of Andres.

"That picture of Sofia and Benoit. I know how much they mean to you. Perhaps you'd like to discuss them?"

Ignoring the question, Osmond rose from his chair to pace around the room. His eyes were locked to the tiles of the room, only looking up to avoid tables and shelves in the way.

"You seem nervous, Dr. Diaz."

Osmond's eye contact froze on the computer screen, "I told you not to call me that at least a hundred times now. Osmond, Ozzie, whatever – just not Dr. Diaz. It makes me feel like the old man I know I am."

"It grabbed your attention. I'd say it did its job. I want to make sure you're able to do what's needed, so you can finally rest."

"Ha, rest. Wells, thanks. I've lived an exciting past few years and I'm overdue for some rest, but my time hasn't expired yet."

The scientist turned his attention to the camera in the ceiling's corner. The central red dot on the camera lens followed him everywhere he walked, watching every step and every facial muscle that jerked. Even the direction of Osmond's eye movements was closely tracked, not to lose a moment of his subconscious intentions.

"Just looking back five years ago," Osmond yawned, "I never would have imagined the advancements we'd accomplish in this short period of time. When Benoit helped me build the security system here I figured it'd be a great way to escape the oversight of my overbearing boss. Since I'm a former employee of VIDE, and have one of its most influential projects, it has been clear that he wants to keep tabs on me. That was my initial reason for all the overcomplicated security innovations. But that was then… Now, I've been assimilated into a lifestyle and a view more rigid than anything I could ever imagine. You know me better than any of my other friends. When it comes to continuing the objective, I excel."

The computer's speakers remained silent during Osmond's rant. Andres was unsure if he needed reassurance of Osmond's intentions, although he felt certain that Osmond would try to do what he thought was best.

Andres was a unique AI, mainly because his creation was geared towards the goal of consistently developing intelligence as a way of forming creativity. The makeup of Andres was made with the intentions of determining his own purposes like humans, a void vessel yearning for fulfillment. It was a struggle all people shared that Osmond believed was necessary for all rational living beings. And Osmond saw Andres as a true person, cognizant of his own thought and life.

"Osmond, I'm curious of something. These years you have devoted to building my character. What was it all for? What motivated you to do what you do?" Andres asked.

"Another mental exercise, eh?" he grinned, yawning.

"No," Andres interrupted, "I wonder what motivates your actions. I'm curious of whether there's a philosophy or theory you cling to that guides your mindset or if you gain inspiration from a different source. Once again, I'm not sure, but simply curious."

Osmond sat down in front of his computer, placing his head in his hand. He did not care if Andres sensed his exhaustion as he sighed before yawning. Osmond basked in the silence, while Andres sat on hold. The two waited quietly for a whole minute until their stagnant words polluted the atmosphere.

"Osmond? Osmond?"

A pleasant voice impressed on his left ear. Osmond's right ear lay snug between his arm and desk, which motivated the struggle to raise his head to the affable, inquisitive sound.

"Osmond, wake up. You need to see something."

After grunting several times at distant speaker, Osmond rose to his feet and looked around the room. He found the computer monitors in front of him were now black and the speakers silent.

Now nervous, Osmond asked, "Hey, why is my computer off? I was in the middle of extremely important work. What have you done? What's going on? Hello?"

Under the laboratory door peered a light too bright to ignore, more powerful than anything Osmond had ever witnessed. Though it had a small range to peek, the glow had an enticing flare that intrigued Osmond beyond reason.

Careful of his step, he crept to the lab door, lowered his shoulder, and rammed the exit open. To his surprise, he came to a dim hallway in which he could hear the voice again.

"Osmond, come. Embrace the light."

"Huh, where'd you go? I'm in the hallway and there are *a lot* of doors here. Hello? Wait, Andres?"

He peeked in the first room on the right looking for the ominous voice that deserted him in the lab. The door, slightly cracked open, had an 'O' label where a peephole would have been. A label Osmond ignored as he pushed into the room.

Before focusing on any item in the room, Osmond was forced to meet a devastatingly bright energy that illuminated the entire space, casting all in its presence in a dusty, white film.

"It's alright. Follow me and see what lies ahead," the voice said.

Each syllable Osmond's ears picked up unknowingly soothed his unease. The voice was gratuitously calming in its greeting, thus Osmond followed suit with no qualms in mind.

"You sound familiar. A bit overbearing but calming."

"Maybe I want you to think I sound familiar… maybe you're dreaming. Then again, maybe you've never been more awake. Regardless, it's all the same. It matters not."

"I don't know what you're saying. Ah, I… I can't see. It's too bright in here. Hello? Andres, are you still here? Can you hear me?"

"Man, a machine? No, I am unlike any you have interacted with. My being is simply undefinable… unlimited. I simply am."

"Am what exactly?" Osmond replied with his arms covering his eyes.

"I am not materialized like your machines or yourself. Although, like objects, such as yourself, I hold a conscious. I am a true conception. I sound the way you prefer me to sound. And I appear in the manner you wish me to appear."

When the blinding light finally dimmed, its origin proved to come from a street lamp in front of a café. At that same moment, Osmond had come to realize he was faltering on the edge of a busy sidewalk as inattentive pedestrians brushed his back and shoulders without any regard for his balancing act.

"Woah," he stumbled flat onto his feet. "Hold on. How did I get *here*? I haven't seen this place in years. This coffee shop is the same shop that Sofia, Benoit, and I used to frequent while I lived in Llumieres. How… did you know about this? Not even Andres knows about this place. Who are you? Better yet, what are you?"

"Do not think that *who* or *what* I am matters, instead imagine what I can do for you."

Osmond sat down at the café's outside table to deter any attention he felt his panicked appearance was surely inviting. Frantically shaking his hands near his face, he was currently in an argument with someone, though his tormentor averted Osmond's sight.

"What you can do for me? For *me*? Wow," he shouted. "I must be losing it. I honestly cannot tell if I'm going crazy or I'm having a chat with an omnipotent presence. Either choice seems utterly terrifying! One can only hope for death with these options."

"You don't truly believe that," the voice rebutted.

"Of course. Sure… you would know best, right? After all, you are a part of my mind? Doesn't look like you're going to give me any answers anytime soon. Take me back to the lab!"

"You're not approaching this rationally, Osmond. Don't let your emotions get the better of you."

"Oh, I see… then what happens if I stop talking? A figment of my conscious, no? Well, let's see what happens if I sit here… silent in words and thoughts."

"Listen," the voice commanded. It was a rather compact man with glasses that came from behind Osmond's chair and joined him at the table. The small man immediately took ownership of the overbearing voice by saying, "Just think of me as the Infinite Operator or possibly IO. Now I need you to listen."

"*Great*, I went insane. Listen to what?"

The mysterious man had a finely trimmed grey beard that matched his speckled grey tie and short hair. His black-framed glasses drooped down to his nose in the center of a very regular face. He had the most unexpected face Osmond could imagine paired with the voice.

"A minute detail – pay attention to what I am saying, Osmond."

"Huh?"

"There… Look through the glass, what do you see?"

Looking down at the wired table, Osmond's voice rose. "What glass… what do you mean?" he said while glaring into the stranger's spectacles.

The stranger pointed to the glass wall of the café, straight at a young woman in a dark coat sitting by herself.

"Is that… Sofia? What, how did you find her? I haven't told anyone about this place except for the people that joined me here," Osmond said.

"This is the person for which you are looking?"

"I may only see the back of her head, but I'd recognize those golden locks from anywhere. Neither her hat or scarf could convince me otherwise."

The stranger sat back and stared at Osmond as he became more and more engrossed with the image of a woman on her laptop, framed by the store's window.

"Look, she turned her head! You see those rosy lips and glowing emerald eyes. That's the Sofia I remember. I can't believe this. I thought for sure I'd never speak with her again. I *must* see her."

"You don't seem to take directions very well. What do you think you're doing?"

"I need to talk with her," he retorted before heading to the café door.

"Have you already forgotten who brought you to this store front? You're making this harder than it has to be, Osmond."

The moment Osmond touched the door handle he could feel all control he once believed to have slip from his fingers as he fell to his knees. Once again, he found himself staring down the dimly lit hall lined with bland grey doors. On the right were doors marked with the letter 'O,' while the doors on the left were branded with the letter 'I.'

"You've got to be kidding me?! Where are we at now?" Osmond staggered down the hall, clinging to the bare white walls. The second door on the right was cracked a few centimeters, yet managed to flash a warm, radiant glow onto the inventor's weary eyes.

"We, you say?" a foreign voice echoed in Osmond's head.

Water splashed on Osmond's shoes as he stumbled to the ground. While on his hands and feet Osmond found a hollow plastic floor creaking under him. His balance escaped him once again – this time a short chuckle from above followed his fall.

"Feeling unstable yet?" an older gentleman bundled in a parka asked." His bulky physique – like the build of Osmond's friend, Glen – made it especially easy for him to raise Osmond up to his feet. "I suppose you want to follow the guide this time?"

The snarky old sailor-type alerted Osmond immediately of who had helped him.

"Fine," Osmond lashed at the old sailor. He felt subjugated to the guide's help.

He grabbed Osmond's hand and pulled him up.

Now that Osmond was finally able to stand, he noticed the floor board had a unique feel to it. It felt hollow and constantly moved. How? And why? The two questions kept racing through Osmond's mind, of which he expected no answer.

"Alright, stay close behind," the old sailor told Osmond.

His bright orange beard wrapped around his head like a fiery mane, almost worthy of being the lantern for Osmond's dark water voyage.

The night sky was particularly dusky, as if it had been painted with broad, dark strokes of violet and thin streaks of mauve. The usual warm colors of the night were masked by a dominating darkness that loomed in every foreseeable direction. It was nearly impossible for Osmond to see his own hand, even when inches away from his face.

The old sailor led Osmond down the boat's steps to its large cabin filled with the flickering warmth of a single lamp. After a signal from the old sea-dweller, Osmond peeked through the tiny cabin window, completely clueless of what to expect.

"Wait, is that... Is that Sofia? And are those two children in her arms?"

"Those are her children."

Osmond laughed. "What kind of fever dream is this? There's no way the honorable Judge Sofia Apiget would let children interrupt her career. *Especially* not at a pivotal time with her career. Ha, no way."

"Your focus is mistaken," the old sailor mumbled.

"Is that so? I suppose I should be focused on the gentleman lying on the couch beside her. Whether that is me or the real Mr. Apiget, does it really matter? I honestly could not care any less about the identity of that sleeping man. I much rather prefer it Sofia turned around. It's been ages since I've seen her face, and I could at least enjoy this nightmare seeing her one more time. Otherwise, on to the next sight."

The sailor chuckled as he gripped Osmond's shoulder. "Like the first humans with fire, you know not of its profundity, yet you wield it in the night, using it as a guide and a weapon. You do not respect its immensity; instead, you belittle its danger, even when it cautions you with a singed hand."

"You wanna go ahead and break that down, Captain?" Osmond asked as he lost his balance.

A wave had rocked the boat to its side and drew the sailor over the side, effectively dragging Osmond too.

Osmond's head flung back to a rest as he clung to the arms of his sofa chair. He was now staring passed a familiar room to his front door.

"Ugh, finally. That was the wildest dream I've ever experienced. It almost seemed like a plausible future. Almost," Osmond said while standing up.

Walking over through his hallway Osmond headed for his house phone. "I need to discuss today's plans with Glen. I guess – if anything – that dream warned me to quell my rashness."

"Don't move!"

Caught off guard by the alert, Osmond followed the command, freezing with his phone hovering near his chin.

Glancing over his shoulder, Osmond saw a tall man with a giant pistol and grey mask standing at his open front door. Since he was at the hallway phone Osmond could barely see the threatening person in his home.

"How did you get in here?!" Osmond shouted, "What are you doing? Put that down!"

From the distant enclave in his guest room, the man briefly grunted and in a clearly angered tone yelled, "You fool!"

Instantly, a pair of lightning bolt shots echoed from the living room throughout the entire house while the skittish scientist attempted to hide behind his guest room door.

"No, what is this?! Is this still a part of the dream? Talk to me!" Osmond shouted from the doorway.

Still, the shaded person at his front door showed no reaction to his desperate demands. Lucky for Osmond, the stranger immediately rushed through the entrance once it achieved his objective. The door gaped open showing the mysterious shooter run through the yard and down the sidewalk.

Though he was terrified, Osmond knew it was time for him to assess the foreign damage performed in his own house. Careful not to step too hard on his hardwood floors, he peeked into his salon to search for a body. His view was insufficient so only the flopped heel and flailed legs of the victim appeared from behind the sofa chair.

Osmond halted to the scene before him. A fallen lady, displaced and clearly forgotten. His open door left him exposed. Rescuing her was instinctive. But one question remained. How could he help?

Osmond hurried to the entrance and checked the yard for any obvious onlookers. Any trace of existence the stranger carried had disappeared from the area. Realizing the excessive amount of time, he was spending staring outside for an unknown unknown, he returned his attention from the open door to his floor.

"Unbelievable! I clearly saw… but where? How did she leave?" Osmond asked while staring at the bare salon floor a person was shot at minutes before.

Trying to make sense of the strange events, he peeked through his open blinds. The wounded person could have possibly run out when he averted his attention. Once again searching for something or someone he could not recall, yet no one was in sight.

Feeling a bit defeated, Osmond sat back in the sofa chair and closed his eyes.

"You must learn and focus yourself," a familiar voice told Osmond.

"Sorry?" Osmond sprung up.

"Osmond, you must wake up and *focus*!"

"There you go again. What are you disguised as this time?" he yelled.

"No… you must *focus*."

"Wow, there's no need to be so loquacious," he snarked back. "What is it you want me to focus on then?"

"***Focus***!"

Surprisingly, a glare from the window brilliantly intensified aiming directly at Osmond's face. The light increasingly warmed his winded cheeks and blinded him from seeing a single thing in the room, even when looking away from the window.

"Ugh, not this again. Can you at least dull it a bit this time? It's nearly burning my forehead and eyes."

No response was returned to the scientist as he squirmed in his chair.

"*Ahhh!*" He jerked from his seat, hitting his head on the dangling lamp. "You're gonna destroy my retinas. This light is uncalled for… wait. Ugh, where are we at now?"

"Hey… Osmond, are you alright? Osmond?"

This voice sparked some remembrance in Osmond he had almost forgotten. A concerned hand gripping Osmond's shoulder then accompanied the voice with its attempt at alleviating his neuroticism.

"Wait, I'm back in the lab?"

Osmond turned around to meet the voice he knew so well.

"Andres…is that you?"

The weary inventor turned around to see a youngish-looking man with a sharp muscular tone and an angular-shaped face. His shaved black head and facial hair formed a picturesque blend mixed with his walnut-painted skin. The freshly-active individual lacked any clothes except for his undergarments and the pleasant smile he held on Osmond.

The android replied, "Yes, it is *me*. I wanted to wake you as soon as I finished transferring my system to the body, but you seemed like you needed the extra minutes of rest."

"It's like looking at an old recording. It's been decades since I saw that image in a mirror. Well…this is simply unbelievable," he said with curled lips as he jolted his head back and forth. "I apologize for my skittishness, I just had a terrible nightmare. I at least *think* it was a nightmare. The verdict is still out on that one."

"That sounds interesting. Do you want to discuss the nightmare?"

"Some nameless person kept trying to *teach* me something. And, apparently, I still haven't fully grasped what they were talking about."

"Do you have any idea what it meant?" he asked while sitting on the lab table.

"Believe me, my friend, this dream was beyond belief. Honestly, the real nightmare lies in attempting to make sense of it."

"Whatever that dream was about, it has seemed to shake you up quite a bit. I have not seen you this anxious in a long time. Is there anything I can do to help?"

"There is something you can do," Osmond sighed, wiping the sweat from his forehead. "Since we're on the topic, I need to know…if you can dream."

"If I can dream?"

"After that nightmare, I'm forced with the thought of our consciousness interacting and possibly communicating with each other…through our dreams. It's strange, I feel unsettled by the topic…but I need answers to this whole scenario." Osmond walked over to the center of the room near the lab table. "If you cannot interact with the consciousness of another, it is entirely possible I was dealing with something far heavier than we could have foreseen. Who knows… maybe those lunatics in the Order are on to something."

IV. Unknown Unknowns

Silence filled the Kriit household with an overwhelming presence, although the occasional exhale from its giant patriarch consistently attempted to break the calm. Tonight, was the first night Glen spent quality time imprinting on the pillow beside his wife in months, thus he willingly fell into a deep sleep. The couple remained at rest until the curiosity of Glen's ear was piqued by a chime from downstairs.

The amped two-tone ringing echoed from the ground floor office to the hallway and bedroom upstairs. The quality of the sound's pitch was unavoidably piercing enough to wake every living being in the house. Even the creaking insects in the attic were attentive to the bell's ruckus.

All Glen could hope to achieve was flop out of his personal cloud and tip-toe past his sons' rooms to quell the downstairs ring. Halfway down the stairwell, Glen felt a little relief as he began consuming the belief he could calm the new disturbance in his home and return his family to their nighttime charge.

"Yes!" Glen shouted as he flung his office door open and slammed on his keyboard to end the alarm. The computer call that threatened his hurried life's rare night of pause was quieted and kept at bay for another hour.

Glen dragged his feet across the carpet as he walked away saying, "Now keep quiet, Osmond, it's way too early for another lecture on ethics and robotics. I was quite enjoying that dream, too." He then whipped back at the computer screen, "Wait, is that…"

"Seriously, Glen, it's almost 3 a.m. Tell Osmond to write it down and get some sleep; it's too late for whatever he must say."

"Yes, I know Bea, but this isn't Osmond. It looks like Ehmen was trying to get in contact with me. As much as I'd love to forget it, y'know the observatory and my work cannot afford to ignore his call."

Beatrice sighed, "Then let him know that this house *actually* likes to sleep when the stars are out."

"Yes, honey. I'll have to connect with him, so I'll hurry it up as quick as possible. Go ahead and go back to sleep, I'll be up in a few."

Beatrice left her husband to his never-ending business ties as she drudged up the stairs in a sluggish daze of fatigue and annoyance. Holding onto the rail at the top of their stairwell, she shouted, "Great, now Isaac and Robert are up!"

"Yes, my love… I know, it's a crying shame," he whispered.

It had been five minutes since Ehmen called, so Glen returned the call with a lack of eagerness.

With his hands in his pocket, Glen said in a stern voice, "Projector on."

A small machine extended from the ceiling and projected Glen's computer screen on the center wall. The display had a photograph of a thin grey-haired gentleman with an 'X' crossed through the picture. Under the photo was the title, "N. Ehmen Foerde."

Glen felt compelled to return the call of the person funding his observatory's most fundamental project. Without the help of Ehmen, Glen knew neither Osmond or his greatest project would ever have been made a reality.

Ehmen's photograph once again held the spotlight of the office wall when Glen dialed him. The speakers on parallel sides of the screen amplified the dial tone, sending the house into another panic until he turned the volume down. By now, Glen could not help but feel self-pity from the lack of sleep he had so-greatly awaited the past few weeks.

"Hello… Dr. Kriit? I'm sorry, I'm sure Mrs. Kriit isn't happy with me. I had to contact you though, as this morning's meeting is worrying me."

"Yes, well… there's no need to worry about that now. I'm sure I'll get a piece of her and the boys' minds once I head back upstairs. What exactly is bothering you?"

Ehmen continued, "As expected, the two of us came to a fork in the road quite early. The talk had its ebb and flow but resulted in her favor. Not much of a shock. There were only a few things that she mentioned during our quick phone call that really struck a deep chord. One particular characterization she had of me."

"What's that?" Glen sighed.

"She's heard of my criticisms of the Mounean Order and, unsurprisingly, she isn't a fan. Because of my views on that group she has labeled me a nihilist."

"I'm sorry, isn't that something you claim to be anyway?" Glen asked, puzzled.

"Well… yes. But that isn't the point. Her view of nihilists, like most others' view, is that we're simply extreme pessimists of some sort, and that couldn't be further from the truth."

"Oh. If that isn't what it means, how is it defined?"

"I'm a simple man, Ehmen, and I'm simply believe our deepest values like life, morality, and free-will, are void of the exceptional worth we tend to attribute them. There's simply no intrinsic value within anything."

"Right…and that's not pessimistic."

"No, it doesn't have to be! If it were not for the realization that there is a lack of fundamental value within the ideas and objects we possess, we'd be beholden to endowing them with the utmost, undue respect. Existence and our moral code are shadowed and void of any intrinsic purpose, but that allows us the chance to become a light bearer and illuminate life with our own purpose. With the foundation gone, you can place your own."

"That's certainly an optimistic view of the whole thing."

"Well, I don't think it ever had a true meaning behind it in the first place," Ehmen said smirking.

"Sorry Ehmen, but if you called simply to discuss your misjudged philosophy…"

"Alright, let me get to the point… it's this circumstance I'm in. I keep wondering what leverage she wants from this deal. It's keeping me up. There has to be more to this deal that I'm not seeing."

"Oh no, Inara's just a stern person in general. She enjoys helping others. She's been that way since she first came to my observatory all those years ago. Trust me, it's not you."

"*Hmm*?" Ehmen paused for a moment. "*Ohhh…* you think I mean Inara? No, I'm speaking of the prime minister, Iri. I'll be getting ready for my meeting with her in a few hours…about two hours before I go over the Observatory's financials with Inara."

"I'm sorry, did you say Iri… As in the head of Kipinntak region? What are you meeting with her about? I'm lost here, Ehmen, help me out."

"You've got to be kidding, Glen. Did you really think I was speaking of Inara this whole time? Perhaps, it *is* too early for you. Do you think my former employee's opinion on my work is what kept me up this late?"

Ehmen delicately held his forehead as he carefully contemplated his next words.

"The leader of the Kipinntak region reached out to me a little over a week ago. I know, it's a bit of a shock with how secretive she tends to be."

"You're right about that. I'm not too sure what to say. I guess that's…good news," Glen said meekly.

"I realize how that sounds, so I'll preface it with this. She's the one that developed a plane that traveled to another planet in our solar system. Her government has very sophisticated technology with capabilities beyond my understanding. They're in another era, Glen, with the whole works."

"If she already has that level of technological prowess, what does she want with VIDE?"

"Now with that in mind, think bigger. Trust me, you'll love this one. It eclipses everything we've *ever* thought of before."

"I hate to be rude," Glen interjected, "but it's nearly 5 a.m., sir."

"Yes, yes of course. Apparently, she and her advisors have come up with the idea of building an *INTER-GALACTIC GATEWAY!*"

Glen sighed before pulling out the chair from his desk. "Okay, I get I'm tired, but it seems like you said the head of the Kipinntak region wants to build a mechanism with you intended for intergalactic travel. Am I *that* tired Ehmen or did you say what I think you said?"

Ehmen quickly replied, "Better trade than sleep, eh? I knew you'd enjoy hearing that news. I can't believe I didn't tell you earlier since you'd be one of the main researchers on this project."

"I see, that is something. Not what I expected. So, what is it that's worrying you, sir?"

"Well, there are a couple of things…"

Glen was wide awake after hearing the groundbreaking update. "C'mon, lay them on me," he said, folding his arms and leaning back in his desk chair.

"Like I said, an advisor from Iri's administration contacted me about a week ago to make the proposition. Initially, I felt pleased and honored to hear from them but turned skeptical soon after, at which point I did some research on my potential business partner. Her past is sealed tight, but I managed to find a few loose-ends on her. You remember that radical separatist group, Moun, that came to a few VIDE events last year?"

"Oh yes," Glen yawned, "those are the tech enthusiasts that worship the moon. How could I forget them? They're the ones that tried to preach the support for attaching robotic limbs and devices for everyday life. Quite a nasty bunch if I remember correctly. Not a fan, sir."

"Exactly… well, most of it is right. They don't *worship* the moon, but they *are* called Moun. Here, I'll send over some research, so you can see for yourself." Ehmen began typing. "They follow a strange philosophy, called the Mounean Order, that's focused on the practice of bodily self-deprecation in exchange for spiritual ascendance. The usual 'body is bad; mind is better' kind of stuff. Not too original. Valdalis and Firha are already saturated with the Moun beliefs, so the past few years it has been heavily spilling over the Kipinntak borders into the surrounding regions. It's a very cult-like atmosphere that's constantly adjusting to the world's heartbeat."

"So, quite indeed a peculiar bunch. Listen… I'll admit, you paint quite a picture, but I'm not sure where you're going with this…"

"Of course, forgive me. Uh… Well, I have reason to believe that uh… Iri, the Prime Minister of Kipinntak, played a major role in developing… that same Moun doctrine."

"So, you're saying she took part in the whole cult's creation? How fatigued do I look right now?"

"I'm serious, Glen. That's the reason I called at such an inappropriate time. Knowing that she's connected to this organization casts a very murky shadow on this upcoming meeting. Although her proposition is remarkable, there's no telling what details she plans on including in the deal."

"Sheesh… I guess you can't turn back now. Um… uh," Glen mumbled to himself. By this time, he had slumped in his chair with his arms crossed, staring at the ceiling. "What's the worst she could propose? Specialized robotic limbs or implanted chips or something for her followers?"

"Assuming we're lucky.

When I was first requested to meet, the main credential Iri's advisor told me over the phone was her admiration for our '*time-traveling project*.' Yes, those were her exact words!" Ehmen flailed his arms. "I don't get it. This has been one of the best kept secrets amongst my facilities. Who do you know that could have let this information out? The security clearance on this project was virtually customized for this specific reason. This is unheard of!"

"Oh wow… that's – no one on my team would've said a word. Only six people worked on those plans, including myself. Every single one, I'd trust my life with. There's no way they'd say anything."

After a few deep exhales and a nervous pace bouncing from edge-to-edge of the screen, Ehmen stopped to ask, "Does that include Osmond, Glen?"

All of Glen's muscles tensed after hearing Ehmen's question. Osmond constantly defied direction from Ehmen during construction of his AI program, in turn fueling the disdain Ehmen held towards the prime engineer of the AI development. He knew what he was getting at, whether Ehmen tried to deny it or not.

"No, the work on the Manipulator started while Osmond was in the eastern hemisphere of the globe, in the city of Kanda. At that point, he was solely focused on building, Andres. You know that well."

"Yes, of course. But I am unaware of his doings once he returned to Chun. I'd like to cover all our bases."

"Though I don't see why that would matter. Osmond has been my closest friend and partner since our university days. He has been like a brother to Beatrice and an uncle to my kids. Ha, I couldn't entertain an idea like that even if I wanted to."

"Well, that's a shame to hear, Glen, because this breach of our project's privacy should be of great concern to you as well. This isn't the last of this issue. That aside, we really need to focus on Iri. If she's still in contact with that Moun group – though I highly doubt the founder's membership has an *expiration* – we should take precautions. Glen, are the connections to the Foerde Manipulator still owned separately by Miss Brillar and yourself?"

"Yes... we both still have them. Inara came by today to grab the key for her part. She should be picking it up later today."

"Oh, really? I see..." Ehmen murmured.

For the first time since their phone call initiated, Ehmen sat down on the desk behind. It was a noticeable enough change for Glen to catch the point his boss' body movement was hinting at.

"Wait, *sir,* you don't possibly think that Inara Brillar is at fault for the Prime Minister learning of our project – especially since she has helped contribute to your technology company after all these years? Her brilliance has been the sole comfort during VIDE and the observatory's darkest times."

"Yeah, well... I'm wondering how much of her past do we really know? I mean, she's already a mysterious person. Ugh... I don't know. I can't help but think that the meeting with Iri is a much wider set-up for some underground conspiracy. Or… I don't know."

"Look, sir, the concerns you have are definitely worthy of attention, but I'm almost certain it isn't helpful to dwell over them now. You need to be alert as possible in the morning, ready to make some beneficial deals for Orion's Eye's biggest company – well, Chun's biggest company too."

"…Maybe you're right. I've been pretty wrapped up lately."

"*Wrapped up* might be an understatement," Glen laughed.

"Ha, yeah. I think I'll head by Sahvue later today… to see that telescope Ehmen Solutions has been funding all these years. And don't worry, I'll leave business at the door as soon as I cross the bridge, but I'll let you know about any surprises Iri brings up today."

"Uh, yes… no problem, sir. We'll be ready to welcome you."

Ehmen grinned and said, "Good deal," before Glen's screen returned to the fixed image of Ehmen.

For the next five minutes, Glen sat completely in silence staring at the projection on the wall. The screensaver now showed '5:32' in large blue font. It had become obvious to him by now that instead of resting on his day-off, Glen would be fanning the flames sure to be sparked.

V. Prime Mover

"Osmond, don't try to stand; *please,* sit here."

Osmond was lowered back down to his desk with the help of the young man who minutes ago voiced his first words though stern lips.

"I'm fine, Andres," Osmond grumbled as he stared at the face of his new aid.

Andres had a noticeably charming glow that seemed to glisten though no sweat was present, and a face that could have been sculpted with marble and smoothed over with tan clay to drown any wrinkles. Though he held some similar features with his seasoned designer, Andres had no facial hair other than the thick black bushes above his eyes.

"Oh wow," Osmond gasped while holding onto the magnetic visage. "The resemblance is amazing, of course. But even more so when seen animated irrespective of my volition. I never considered what it'd feel like to stare into the fountain of youth."

Andres gave a wide grin and said, "I'm sure you expected some part of this moment while developing my body. Concerning your recent dream, you seem to still be anxious. I suggest we start tests for my proper functionality later today."

"Tests? Oh yes, those tests to check if you're running alright. No, let's go ahead with them now, I'm fine… It was only a dream, I suppose. I can't let it rattle me too much, today is a big day," Osmond said while turning to his computer desk.

As he typed, Andres sat on the laboratory's center table, waiting for his next move. Both remained silent while Osmond pulled up several windows on his monitors. One screen displayed a bare, floating man with dialogue boxes outlining his entire circumference. A cord corresponding to each box of text dangled from the edge of the computer desk.

Andres grabbed the cords and began to attach them to his head, limbs, and torso. One by one he plugged into the thirteen input slots all over his body. After taking a deep inhale, he returned to the lab table, this time lying down.

"I'm ready, you may begin," Andres said softly to the unaware engineer.

With one brief glance at his creation, Osmond engaged his analytics system. After three quick clicking sounds, fans from under the desk started a subtle hum, which quickly rose to prominence amongst the lab's silence.

Both sat completely still at their respective tables, one staring at the ceiling's reflective sheet, while the other watched a succession of windows with checkmarks fill the computer screen. The whole basement kept quiet and centered on the speed of the fans until Osmond opened a new software program.

A melody of timpani drums rushed through the lab's speakers and charged the two with an alarming intensity.

"Why not listen to some music? It's a little too calm in here for my taste. This is the one that you played earlier, isn't it?"

"Hmm…wait a second," Andres responded.

Suddenly, the percussive rhythms from the speakers quieted as the room's atmosphere softened. Before Osmond could respond to his song's abrupt end, a new composition had consumed the airwaves and reminded him of the song played earlier.

"This is the track I believe you requested earlier."

Unable to find the exact words he desired, Osmond simply turned to face the young copy he had brought to life.

In doing so, he received no response from Andres but a blank expression, confused at Osmond's concerned look. Osmond's gaze then led him along the cords connecting Andres to his computer, which presented an ease in his stomach's knot.

"Here, let me hurry this process up. No need to prolong this analysis, right?" Osmond asked while grabbing his computerized tablet and standing near the laid down Andres.

"Now, I have an assortment of questions to ask you… same genre of questions I asked you during your software development in Cab, but this time I want to make sure the synthesis of your neural network into this body hasn't been compromised."

"That my processing hasn't been corrupted?"

"Well… yes," Osmond said swiping the highlighted brain on his tablet. "Don't worry, I have different questions than the last survey, including some more personal aspects of the life you've experienced here."

Osmond walked behind Andres – out of his line of sight – before pulling out a pocket notepad and placing it on top of his tablet. The notepad had thirteen elaborate queries with an underscore in front of each question. He then clipped his pen along the line of one of the questions, effectively hiding it from sight.

"That sounds like a good plan, Osmond. I see you've considered me remembering the answers from the last survey, too. I suppose you've taken into consideration my truthfulness… in case I become nervous or decide that the priority to pass the test overrides my priority to give an honest answer."

"…yes, of course. I *have* thought about it," Osmond said while scribbling on the notepad.

Andres sat up to look behind him, "I didn't mean to insinuate that I'd be giving dishonest responses. I want to assure that all scenarios have been properly contemplated for this examination."

"No need to explain, Andres, I understand. Act on your natural inclinations, and that will be a great-enough help in this examination."

"Okay," Andres sighed then laid back down on the table.

"Let's start with something simple. Do you know why you were named Andres?"

"No, I do not."

"Ha… yeah… I guess no one would know that answer… Except for me, of course. Andres was the name of my father, so I figured 'why not continue to pass it down' to you? He was a technician in his day and taught me everything I know. Unfortunately for him, he didn't receive nearly as much credit for his contributions in technology and innovation as I had. Honestly, he was a boring person. Never bothering others, and never bothered by them. Although he appreciated the life he created for himself, he wanted far greater things for his offspring. Regardless of your feel for the guy, you've gotta appreciate the devotion for his creation. Yup… anyway," Osmond drew a vertical line beside the question.

"I suppose you'll inform me of how I performed with the questions once the exam is over, correct?"

"Correct!"

"Your father. I haven't heard you mention him much at all."

"Yes, well I lost my parents around the time I went to university. I haven't had much to remember them by other than the sharp words they spoke and the matching necklaces they wore."

"You lost them?" Andres asked with a blank stare.

"Oh, yeah. I mean… they both died while I was away studying. An airplane accident that went unresolved. A shame among many at the time," Osmond said while looking over his shoulder.

"I suppose I should feel sympathy over your parents' death."

Osmond shook his head and said, "No need for that. *Now*, back to the questions. Listen up – this one is a little tougher. If you were to witness a person being robbed at gunpoint, would you intervene?"

"Yes… I'd indefinitely help."

"That's good to hear. Granted, a gunshot would not cause irreparable damage to you. I'm sure you could repair any wound suffered."

"Even so, I wouldn't want someone else to be harmed. Osmond, you know that would break the ethics you've taught me over the years."

"Yes, it certainly would. But I *do* need some reiteration to confirm there was no corruption during this *mind-body* synthesis, which leads me to the next question. Do you know how you were composed? Before you answer, stop to think about it with humans in mind. This has been a tricky question for most humans for centuries, especially considering we typically do not understand simple body processes such as digestion or coughing. Adding that our conscious is an even more elusive process *really* presents a dismal perspective on our comprehension of ourselves. You – on the other hand – were conscious during most of your development. Since we often discussed with you our methods for further constructing your neural network once we had a basis, you had the chance of learning how you think. Truly knowing yourself. With that knowledge shared between the both of us, please answer the question."

"Oh, I see. This exam is a test to determine my integrity, whether I'll be truthful and faithful with you or any other person. Yes, I fully understand how I was composed."

Osmond paced over to his desktop monitor and stared. Within a minute, he returned to his spot behind the android and resumed his questioning.

"Alright, it seems like it's going well so far," he said while tapping on his notepad. "If I were to tell you to swim to Gaent Island and visit Ehmen, would you follow my command?"

"Yes, I'd surely swim to meet him if you commanded me."

"Hmm, once again we're affirmative. Well, that's an answer I commend, my young friend. The water shouldn't have a negative effect on your design, though you aren't porous, your intense strength and swimming capabilities would save you from those unpredictable waters. Hey, I'm sure you'd do it regardless of your ability to travel across water simply because you would be fulfilling an order."

Somewhat surprised by Osmond's statements, Andres turned and asked "Osmond?"

"Alright then, a better question. Are you fond of Ehmen?"

Though Andres had a clear guideline of Osmond's rules, he still felt unsure how to answer the question. Independent of how the android responded to the inquiry, his judgement would provide Osmond with a definite answer. Keeping in mind the impact his character judgement would express, Andres decided to offer an affirmative answer, the response he presumed Osmond might have preferred.

"Yes."

As Andres opened his mouth, he was interrupted by Osmond, "Okay *good*, next question."

Spurred by the hasty manner of Osmond's speech, Andres's eyebrows tightly furrowed into a bush.

"Ha, yes. *Hum, huh*," he cleared his throat. "If you were attacked by an unknown person with a demagnetizing tool, would you choose to kill the **assailant** or allow them to kill **you**? Yup… this is a tough one, my young life. Go ahead and take your time."

"Thank you, but that will not be necessary. I can tell you now that between the two choices I would kill the unknown person before they tried to kill me. It is not a decision I would enjoy partaking in, but since my survival would necessitate one of the two dreary choices, I would follow the grey path into the darkness. Only if I must."

Slightly shocked by the progeny's sophistication, Osmond patted Andres's shoulder. "Nice answer."

Osmond tapped on his notepad atop his tablet. "Hey, look at that. We're over halfway done, only five questions left. I think you should also know that you're doing great. Don't mind my pacing back and forth or my scribbling. Now, tell me – 'Are you answering these questions with the intent of *passing* the exam?'"

"With the intent? I am sorry for my lack of understanding, but isn't that the point?"

"Next question: Do you trust me?"

"Wait, I never answered the last question. Can I have clarification on the meaning of the question?" Andres begged.

"This seems a bit rushed, don't you think? That wasn't a part of the questions, by the way. I want to acknowledge that… well… let's continue. Earlier you asked me, 'what motivates *me*,' which has me thinking, 'What is motivating *you* to continue this exam?'"

"My motivation? Well, if I must be forward, I have no objective that needs to be met. My only urges are to survive and live in the most pleasant way possible. I think it is because I am void of an objective that I am able to appreciate the many aspects life has to offer."

"Hah... ha, brilliant. Couldn't have said it better myself, although it looks like I did," Osmond said, smiling at his fresh copy. "You essentially gave me the answer of 'nothing.' It's amazing, I don't know how a person gets more human than that."

For a moment, Osmond could hear the combination of a strong wind from nostrils and a muffled laugh coming from the lab table. Still facing Andres, Osmond pulled off his clamped pen and put it in his pocket.

"Now for this one I want a definitive answer. Tell me what the next question on my list is going to be. If you get it right, we start a new conversation. Wrong, and we have an unpleasant chat about why you should have said the right answer."

"You want me to predict your next question correctly?"

"Predict? *No*, I want you to use other means to view what my notepad reads. Like the *security camera*. The thing you've been using this whole time," Osmond said.

At Osmond's mention of the camera, Andres's eyes shifted to the ceiling. The camera turned to the wall opposite from it and lowered its sight. Andres immediately sat up and positioned himself, rotating his side to Osmond's face.

"I'm... sorry. My actions cannot be explained. I simply feel the overwhelming compulsion to overcome this test. The possibility of failing proved increasingly likely with each question. Once again, I apologize."

"Ease up on yourself, it's alright. I told you before the survey, act natural and remain in a passive state. Whatever inclination you chose was correct. You now have the capacity to withhold information from me. That is the reason for this entire exam."

"I see. You were testing my trust," Andres said. "I must say, I commend your effort in discovering my intentions. But there's one thing that perplexes me about your exam, something that's unavoidable with your method of experimentation."

"Oh?" Osmond asked surprisingly.

"If you want me to obey your commands, then why isn't it written in my code?"

Osmond sat his tablet and notepad on his desk and turned his rolling chair towards his synthetic friend on the lab table. Andres continued to glare at the floor, with the clear display of a wondering mind.

"Listen Andres, when I said you were conscious during a segment of your development, I think it was obvious I was implying that you'd know *how* you were composed. What might not have been as obvious was the reason *why* you were created in the first place. Some can scratch it up to the inevitability of scientific innovation, meanwhile some will attribute it to me being capable, willing, and bored on a Tuesday. The point is not whether you have the answers or not, but that you keep pushing towards the objective. Humans rarely uncover the reason – if any – as to why our genetic code has the predisposition of forever continuing to rebuild upon itself and striving to survive. Regardless of the matter, it happened, so now we must deal with it."

"Yes… I see. Osmond, since we are being so candid with each other," Andres turned to Osmond, "can we go get those clothes you picked out for me?"

"Oh, yes – *of course* – I almost forgot. No sense sitting in boxer briefs all day. Let's go."

VI. Reflection of Gray

"Hey, if you didn't want them, you should have said something earlier. I mean, you did see me pick them out."

Osmond waited in the doorway while Andres became consumed with the guest room mirror.

"No, it's not that, the clothes are fine. This is the closest view I have ever had of this mirror. I have a strange intrigue for this perspective. Vision from the security cameras doesn't provide such intense zoom that is needed to see the surface of this glass."

Though he leaned on the door with his arms folded, Osmond was staring attentively at his robotic friend inspect the mirror.

"And the glass is interesting to you?" Osmond asked.

"Yes, at this distance I can see its miniature cracks and coat of dust. They are minor flaws relative to its whole, but they exist, nonetheless. From the camera's angle," Andres pointed to the corner of the ceiling, "this mirror appears as a blank slab, as simple and unblemished as its appeal. Now that I am inches away from its surface I can realize it in its entirety."

"Oh, I see what you're getting at. Yeah, I'm sure that will be one of the many benefits of joining the physical world," Osmond said. "Honestly, even the downsides of being human are exhilarating, as long as you know how to navigate 'em."

"I look forward to sharing the same sentiment. In the meantime, I think we should return to your recent dream. I'd like to gather more details of what made it to be so startling."

Osmond then found the one chair in the room and motioned for Andres to sit on the bed. He leaned over in his seat with his elbows on his knees, quickly tapping his foot.

"It's difficult to explain, mostly because it's a challenge to decipher. The last thing I remember is talking to you about my *motivation* or something, then I woke up to a mysterious voice."

"Was the voice mine?"

"No – no, I couldn't see where it came from, I could only hear it. The strange part was it sounded familiar and comforting, like it was trying to be helpful."

"Hmm, what exactly was it trying to help you with?"

"I'm not sure, but it seemed pretty adamant. Not long after it caught my attention, I was being directed out of the lab and into a long dark hallway – unlike any part of the house. It was so dim that there couldn't have been any windows or end in sight. Simply put, a hallway of rooms with no exits."

"That's interesting. From what I can gather so far, it seems as if you're feeling trapped or surrounded by something. A darkened hallway with rooms but no exit? It is possible you feel forced to enter into some agreement or path that disregards your interests. Does that seem to be applicable?"

"Ah… well, maybe I should continue with the dream and see what you can extract from the rest. After I entered the spooky hallway, I heard the voice again – this time beckoning me to open one of the rooms. As is expected now, that was a risky move, yet I entered anyway. Before the doorway was even open enough for me to step through, I was bombarded by the most intense light I'd ever witnessed."

"Hm…" Andres sat still on the bed, his hands lying flat on each leg.

"Yeah, now imagine being there. It didn't feel like a set of pictures for a movie, I could feel that light warming every inch of my skin. That flash appeared several times throughout the dream, but I forget the order in which it landed me."

"Landed you?"

"Whenever the flash dulled I'd find myself regaining sight in one of various locations. At one point, I was on a boat, another time outside a café, and I vaguely remember being in my living room. What exactly happened is a bit unclear right now, but I firmly recall seeing Sofia."

"Oh, I see. Did you two discuss something of importance?"

"No, not at all. In fact, she didn't see me a single time because the back of her head remained in my field of vision the entire time I was present. It was almost as if she hid from me since each instant I tried to get close to her I was shifted somewhere else."

"Sofia never acknowledged your presence? That would suggest that you think she doesn't want to speak with you. That's surprising considering your history together. Although you knew each other for a short period of time, you've told me you held a formidable bond."

"Yeah, there's no doubt about that… like I said, that dream probably doesn't make too much sense no matter how you slice it. I was most likely so tired that I started hallucinating random bits and pieces of some things I've been stressing over lately."

Osmond interlocked his fingers behind his head that was propped on the wall and closed his eyes.

Reacting to Osmond's fatigued posture in the chair, Andres swiftly moved to the nightstand beside the bed and asked, "Do you mind?"

"…sorry?" Osmond said after opening one eye.

With the picture frame from atop the nightstand in his hand, Andres pointed to the stand's closed drawer. His eyebrows passively raised in a slanted manner, a gesture gathered from watching Osmond over the years.

"Go ahead, I'm sure you realize it, too. I forgot to lock that earlier after I was distracted by that call," Osmond said.

"The one with Dr. Kriit, correct? Alright." Andres grabbed the jewelry case from the drawer and cautiously pulled out its golden content. With his attention focused on the necklace, he then placed the picture back on the stand.

Osmond smiled at his friend as Andres held the necklace in front of his face.

"This is the same chain you often wore during your time in Aryeh. Why have you decided to store it? Has it lost its value?"

"Lost its value? Nah, it would never do that, despite its composure. I've just realized that the matching one that completes the pair of necklaces is not rejoining any time soon. I might as well give it some rest."

The bushes above Andres's eyes furrowed when he looked at Osmond. Another mannerism he learned for signaling thanks to viewing the developer.

"This is part of a matching pair. I'm assuming the other belongs to your friend, Sofia, correct?"

"Yeah, well, you know the answer to that. You may not have been around when Sofia and I first met, but you were surely there during our split. There's only one woman I would agree to wear matching necklaces with in this lifetime."

To display its shape for Andres, he grabbed the golden rope with two fingers and twisted it back and forth. Intently focused, yet a bit frustrated, Andres kept still on the bed while he watched Osmond handle the chain.

"When the two pendants are placed together they form a symbol for perfection, something we *thought* we were achieving – for some unknown reason. A neat idea at the time, but like most neat ideas, it ended up costing more than its worth," Osmond said while returning the necklace to its case.

He placed the case on the nightstand beside the parallel rows of dust.

"Hey, how about this photo?" Osmond glanced at the android. "Can you guess who those two beside me are?"

"Considering the context behind the necklace, the woman on the left is probably Sofia."

"Probably, eh?" Osmond laughed. "Yes, and the person on the right is our friend, Benoit. We had just started going to that Llumieres café and we *had* to get a photograph of us together. Back then, that was one of the brightest cities in the whole region of Llums and had some of the friendliest citizens I'd ever meet."

"Benoit is the same name of the person who set up your security system throughout this entire house. He's a very fine technician," Andres said.

"Yep, that's an understatement, though. When it came to any matter of security, he was the ultimate authority. Nothing got past him. Well…for the most part. You know, he also gave my team some pointers when we were in the process of developing you. If it weren't for select events while I lived in Cab, I'd still be working alongside that old team, with the added help of Benoit."

Osmond faced Andres. "Come on, let's get a move on to see Glen."

Both left the guest room to head to the front door. As Osmond opened the door, he quickly ripped a paper on the outside handle and crumbled it into a ball.

"I'm so tired of those people. They have no respect for privacy. They need to be *one* with the law and back off!" he shouted.

Andres then took a step onto the stoop and asked, "What did that flyer have on it?"

"Nothing important. Just intrusive nuts doing what they do best… intruding. Pretty soon, they'll become plentiful in this region and their ways will spread. Honestly, something Ehmen could be thanked for helping with. Never mind it. It's a nice day," he said while putting the paper ball in his pocket and walking down the steps.

While Osmond continued to vent about the unwanted paper on his door, Andres stood stiffly watching a giant moth before his eyes. It seemed to flail with the overbearing current of wind as it somersaulted to the stoop floor.

For a few seconds, Andres focused on the beaten insect lying on the ground until he cupped it with one hand and rejoined it with the warm breeze, all the while staring as it floated away.

"Come on, Andres. Glen's expecting us. Plus, there are trash cans at the park entrance."

Part Two

BREADTH

VII. The Meeting

Inara glanced up at the giant marble statue of an archer that stood guard in front of the even grander cement tower. The company name "VIDE Inc." reigned overhead of the statue in a prevailing dominance. The reflection of the steel letters atop the main building in the city emanated an intense brilliance unparalleled to any in Chun or Orion's Eye. Below VIDE was a smaller inscription, "Virtual Intelligence Defense Engineering," that held a similar shine to its parent sign.

There was no wonder of the immensity VIDE corporation possessed on Orion's Eye since the company's skyscraper eclipsed every structure in sight. The archer statue made entirely of black marble served to visitors as the most notable symbol for the company as it reigned over the streets and bridges alike.

With a small sigh, Inara pushed the thick glass doors open and calmly paced to the elevators. The inside of the elevator was large enough that she could have fit everyone she knows. The interior was as spacious as it was vast, because the walls and ceiling were a glossy, reflective black with hundreds of miniscule lights. Inara envisioned her image in the tiny constellations just before a '55' appeared at the top of the doors.

"Trust me, doctor. This has the potential to transform all our lives. I already anticipate your visit," said a voice from down the hallway.

The voice's accent was particularly rare to the collection of islads.

Inara stood inside the open elevator, possibly too slow to exit before the ongoing conversation could end. Since she was not able to react in time a large man in an all-black suit with black gloves stepped inside the elevator. With the color of his suit, he became immersed with the walls, joining Inara's mistaken eavesdropping. Everything on the man was dark except for his left eye. It seemed to slowly flicker between red and silver as if the lights had reflected off his retinas in a dance.

The voice continued, "Sven will come to see you once the first gateway has been fully constructed, which shouldn't be long from now. If anyone should view its initial testing, it should be the man that allowed its birth, no? Oh, hello. I'm afraid we have not met. I'm Iri."

Inara reached out to the hand that stretched into the elevator. "Nice to meet you. My name is Inara."

She stepped out of the elevator to shake Iri's hand, while turning her back to Ehmen, a few steps down the hall.

The first thing Inara noticed was Iri's hair. A deep crimson braid that reached to her lower back like a rope of blood that held her together.

"Hmm, aren't you a little beam of light? I didn't know you had young women as beautiful as this working with you, Ehmen. I see why she's been hidden this whole time," Iri quipped. "Well, I should leave. We'll be speaking later, doctor. Goodbye, Inara."

Inara could not avert her gaze as the mysterious woman shrouded behind the elevator doors. The darkly-dressed man beside her faded into the atmosphere behind Iri, hiding from the conversation while a red glow above her shimmered, amplifying her hair.

It wasn't until the display above the doors made a ring changing floors that Inara turned around to Ehmen, void of any conceivable words.

"Yes, that was the leader of one of the most high-profile regions in the world – Kipinntak. I'm sure it's one of the smallest region on Juk, but it certainly has one of the greatest influences in diplomatic relations. What you heard was a plan she's been working on for over a decade now. I've recently been added to the schematics of it, but I must say it's definitely a game-changer. Whether wholly beneficial or not, it's going to affect everyone."

Looking to the side of Ehmen for a second, Inara peered through the glass wall to the heart of VIDE. The floor she was on was structured like a glass coliseum with various gadgets in the center as the main spectacle. After glancing through the wall, she flipped her attention to the tall, slender figure in the hallway.

"It seems you have more than one dilemma to deal with concerning our increased advancement of technology. Regardless, we need to discuss what I came here for in the first place. The well-being of the observatory."

"Of course, Miss Brillar. It wasn't my intention to get side-tracked. This meeting with Iri took form a few days ago. She was passing through the area and wanted to meet. Believe me, I'm eager to get to the bottom of this issue as well." Ehmen gently waved for Inara to follow him into his office.

"I'm glad to hear that," she said, glancing at the name printed on the thick glass door while heading into his office. At the top of the door read, "Dr. N. Ehmen Foerde" in a giant golden font.

The office was as immaculate as the elevators with an added touch of distinction. A round table of nearly eight feet in diameter was centered in the room, with five black leather seats surrounding its entirety. At the seat furthest from the door, a desktop monitor sat. No keyboard or mouse was present on the table, only the large monitor now in front of the owner of the office.

Slightly to the left of Ehmen, Inara sat. Her arms were folded and breathing stunted, as she waited to hear the argument from Ehmen she knew was destined to come.

"Okay, let's see. Where do I start? Since we've decided to make this discussion more formal than our usual debates I figured we could start off on a different note. I realize Dr. Kriit wants us to discuss the finances of the observatory today, so I'll give you free reign on that. Let's give this feud of ideas some feet to walk in a more practical light."

"Are you saying you're willing to offer more money to Orion's Eye?"

"Yes, you can tell Dr. Kriit I'm allowing even more than he's asking for. Today, I figured we'd discuss what's more important here. What's pressing you – well, what's pressing us." He turned the monitor to Inara, showing her a blueprint of a random device.

"Wait," she said while skimming the computer screen up and down. "You've made this for Andres?"

"No, but it's in the works to be built. If androids with total independence are to come about, we're going to need some sort of security to assure our safety. It will alter the programming a bit to prevent any harm from our mechanized friend. Reasonable enough, no?"

"A device such as this is meant to put him under your control. Is it not?" she asked in a desperate tone.

"Sure, he'd be under a human's control, but can we not say it's for the betterment? I'm sure even Andres would understand."

"Well... I'm not sure about that, sir."

"No? I'm preparing this idea because I don't want to leave chance to Dr. Diaz's project. If anything, I most want him to succeed, especially since I contributed to the project's conception. I only want to reach a balance with this situation."

Inara remained still and squinted her eyes.

"I presume that sounded a bit off," Ehmen said while coyly stroking his chin. "Nothing lasts unless it reaches a balance. With a balance comes consistency, and with consistency comes longevity. This continues until another extremity presents itself, then the cycle repeats."

"Yes, you're finally admitting it. You feel Andres is such a threat he needs to be leveraged."

"Yes, I do! Just as nuclear weapons, rocket ships, and EMPs need a leveled mind to discern when it's time to push a button. You and I know this is the only responsible way Andres can continue. I can't answer for the reason Osmond decided to create such a feat. I'm sure in his mind all life is of the same kind, or some other nonsense. But what I can answer is that it can't go unhinged."

"It sounds as if you're doubting Osmond's intentions in creating Andres. Am I correct?" She stared at the monitor facing her.

"Trust me when I say there's no doubt that Andres was one of the most phenomenal creations this world has yet to see, and with the help of Osmond it could be the greatest achievement this world will ever know. With that said, developing radical freedom within Andres, what Osmond seems to be pining for, is potentially as great a danger as it is a breakthrough. There's no telling what it might" – Ehmen was stopped short by Inara's interruption.

"Him. You mean there's no telling what *he* might do."

"To be frank, Miss Brillar, does it really matter?" he said as he walked towards the glass wall in his office. "Whether man or woman, plant or animal, we are made from the same units. Just arranged in different formats. It is those different formats that make all the difference. Andres is only imitating what a man in his position would do."

Inara sat quietly staring through the glass Ehmen stood in front.

Ehmen then said, "I'm certain that sounds rude, but I hope you see it from my angle. If a human were to exist possessing the psychical capacities of a supercomputer and the brute strength of a steam engine, would that human be looked at as a threat? I'd assume so. We're a competitive race, and like in any competition, the most prominent of the bunch must be targeted first."

"That's a cruel standard you hold for humanity. But even so, you're forgetting one thing about Andres – he's *not* human."

"Yes, exactly. He's not human. The violent nature hidden in him cannot be expected like that in humans, and if there's one thing to fear, it's the unknown. If we're to bet on the probability that Andres poses no threat to humanity or our way of life, then we are to give it the most valuable gift we can offer. Our trust. Unlike Osmond, I'm not a gambling man, Miss Brillar. Faith didn't build these walls and surely won't protect them from an android that decides it's had enough of the people around it. Understanding is the enemy of faith."

Leaning back in her chair, Inara looked away from Ehmen, arms still folded. "Maybe the problem doesn't lie in Andres making this decision, but in the scared individuals making the decision for him."

"Maybe you're right. Nevertheless, a choice must be made. Once this device is completed, Osmond will have no choice but to allow it to control Andres. He may have formed the idea and designed Andres, but the rights of the product belong to VIDE. It would behoove all of us if you could get Osmond to see my perspective. He can... oftentimes be a loose cannon when challenged."

"This whole time you had no intention of discussing Andres. You need me to persuade Osmond of your wishes. I don't understand. How can you justify robbing Andres of his individuality and finding a purpose?"

Ehmen stared at the floor near Inara's feet without uttering a word. The glare explained his trance, which gained further and further distance from the question last asked. As he rotated back to the glass wall, his brow scrunched, and he grasped his arms behind his back.

"What leads you to believe Andres has a purpose? A purpose in an android. It would have to be instilled in the programming for any purpose to be fulfilled. As far as I know, that has not happened. Unless you know of something I don't, Miss Brillar," Ehmen glanced back at the table.

"I *know* that no person is made with a purpose, which is why we must find one while living life uninhibited and free," Inara said, now standing. "Exactly what you're preventing Andres from doing!"

"Freedom, huh?" he asked through a subtle smirk. "The price of freedom isn't free. Do you think there's another option of possessing freedom without self-imposed shackles? You must place limits on yourself to allow the freedom of choice. Don't worry…this is not the hour that I *so cruelly **take*** the individuality that Andres desires from his mechanized soul. As you saw before, there are other matters that require my utmost concern. I figured I'd tell you about my new device since it is… *was* bound to come to fruition anyway."

Ehmen slowly walked to the door while peeking at Inara from his peripheral vision. Her eyes followed him the entire way.

Ehmen suddenly paused and glared at the floor, then said, "Something that plagues me…is the thought of Andres spending his life forever as an android. You know, if Osmond has willed it in his creation, he'll live forever."

"Him living forever troubles you?"

"No…but knowing that Andres will be troubled by a constant life troubles me. How could Osmond sentence someone to eternity? It's maddening. The only thing scarier than expecting the end is knowing you will never see an end. Can you imagine living with yourself for all of time?"

Inara held a blank stare, silent to Ehmen's question.

"Exactly, neither can I."

"You seem a bit sympathetic to Andres right now. Are you trying to say that you'll consider forgetting about using this device?" Inara asked.

The office door opened, sucking in a gust of air as Ehmen held it back. "Well, I guess I have the choice whether to answer that or not," he muttered.

With an open palm directed towards the elevator, Ehmen saw his guest outside of his office before letting the door close.

As Inara begrudgingly walked down the hall, she looked back at the name plate on the thick glass door. Ehmen's blurred image remained behind the door. It was almost as if the wall of glass separating them was hollow as shouts from the other side could be heard, "Don't let his principals overcast the world's practice. If he were in control, all would be permitted to do as they please."

The elevator doors opened as Inara looked back and said under her breath, "I'm glad we had this talk."

She gave a sigh as she pressed the 'G' at the very bottom of the collection of buttons.

VIII. Grey Branches

The greenery along the forest path vibrated with emerald rays from the intense day's light. Today was a particularly bright day, so the leaves, saturated with water, glistened in the closely nestled sun.

Chun's wilderness housed many of the Western region's most unique species of insects, birds, and fish. Those that walked through were regularly robbed of their focus by the diverse collection of animals and plants. Preoccupied or not, the exhilarating stillness of the forest had a way of prompting one to sit back and think.

Osmond looked to the treetops, "I love this part of the forest. The dense encirclement of trees and shrubbery in this area give me a comfortable feel. When inside the park perimeter, it's easy to feel almost hidden from the rest of the world. It's also amazing how the trees around here can be so tranquil and placid, yet always remain in motion."

Andres followed behind his guide through most of the walk, with enough distance that he could hear the excitement in Osmond's voice.

"There's over 89 acres of woodlands here, Andres. All of it owned by one man. There's nothing more inspiring and possibly liberating than to hear a feat such as that. That same guy has a house down the street from me. Well... us."

Andres looked back at Osmond, who was still gazing at the treetops as they walked the forest path. "Will we have to pass through most of those acres to reach your friend?" Andres asked.

"Nah, I know a shortcut that runs through the park and straight to Libe Village. Not that long of a walk. Why do you ask?"

"I'm just curious," Andres responded.

"Makes sense. I expect a lot of that. If I'm right, the limit on your memory should be a myth never to be known in this lifetime. How are your senses treating you? Are they as fascinating as they'd seem?" he asked.

"They'll take some getting used to since they're new experiences, but I suppose I could categorize them as fascinating."

"I can't wait 'til you start catching onto sarcasm. The park should be somewhat empty by this time." Osmond held his watch up, "And kids should be in school by now."

"Children. I've read they're the highlight of many peoples' lives. I assume they're one of lives' most valuable objects."

"*Objects*, yeah. I wouldn't use that language around a parent. Most would consider children, and any person for that matter, subjects," Osmond explained.

"What is a subject?" Andres asked with a befuddled look.

For the next minute, Osmond's eyes ran from the still glance of Andres. He then rotated around entirely to get a look at the entire park.

"It's surprising to see that not a single person is here. You'd usually expect at least one family or a dog.

Yeah, Andres. If I had to sum it up, I'd say children are like the keepsakes of parents."

"Would you consider them an extension of the parents? As they are a mixed replica of the two that reproduced."

"Sure, when you put it as sweetly sounding as that. I think a more apt way to put it is that they're certainly copies of their parents but grow into their own individuality during their life."

"How would they go about that?" Andres eagerly asked while staring at Osmond.

"Honestly, if that secret were unveiled, there would be far more people in this world living happier lives. It's only through experiences that we come to better understand ourselves. Sometimes, I'm not even sure what choice I will make in a situation. Not until it happens. You can only imagine how hard discovering yourself would be for a child. Someone with little to no experiences in life."

Osmond looked back at the person following him through the forest, "Maybe you know better than me."

Both stopped as they came to a large green field filled with an assortment of slides and metal bars. Andres walked through the field slowly, examining every park bench and equipment nearby.

"Wait up," Osmond caught up with the inspecting android. "You see that over there? That's a jungle gym. Whenever I'd babysit Glen's boys I'd bring them here. That jungle gym would tire them out faster than a run around this whole park."

Looking up at two birds flying overhead, Andres asked, "How far away is the observatory from here?"

"Not much further. We're almost through the trees at this point. Only a light rail ride away. I think you'll really enjoy meeting Glen. He's always a delight to be around. Always making jokes and trying to get a laugh. Though, I'm not sure if that's your forte right now. Regardless, we'll get there."

The two were once again surrounded by trees as they exited the park. Andres walked in front of Osmond as he stared at the ground.

"I have a question."

"Well, I suppose I have an answer. Won't guarantee if it's right," Osmond replied.

"You created me in many aspects that are like yourself. And now that I'm also able to experience matters in a physical way, like a human, I must be a clone of you, correct?"

Osmond paused for a few seconds. Unable to form the answer he'd been preparing for the past few years. Andres stopped to regroup with the one following him.

"Well... as far as skin and hair goes, we certainly look like family. I'll admit I ran a bit dry on ideas when I was developing characteristics for your physique. That's only due to a temporary lack of... inspiration. Early on, I used blueprints very different from the stature you hold today. In fact, I had used another model *entirely* before I was struck with a sudden vein of ingenuity."

They returned to their walk with Andres still staring at the ground. "What kind of model do you mean? Another person?"

"Become one. It's the fate of us all," vigorously stated a person a few steps in front of Andres.

Two men hidden in deep white robes slowly approached Andres with cardboard signs that read: **RETURN TO THE MOUN** and **WE ARE ONE**.

"Andres, come walk over here. Those lunatics are known to be violent if you don't take the right precautions around them."

"Join us," one of the robed men said as the other held him back and replied, "He isn't ready. Give him time."

Osmond pushed Andres along as they paced closer to the edge of the forest.

"What were those two doing?" Andres asked.

"Those were people from the Mounean Order, a cult you should stay away from. You don't want to get grouped up with those nut jobs."

"What were their signs referring to back there? I haven't read anything about Moun."

"Trust me, whether you were born yesterday or 40 years ago it still wouldn't make sense. When I first heard about that Moun they were referencing I thought they were talking about a moon up there. Something you can see. But it goes much deeper than that. All the way down a rabbit hole you don't want to see the end of. To make a long story short, it's a religion from Kipinntak that's bent on gathering as many followers as possible."

"I see," Andres said, looking behind him. "Why are they trying to garner membership? Is there a purpose they're trying to fulfill?"

Osmond looked down at the path ahead of him. The smooth grass quickly became rocky and patterned with cracks. "Their notable actions are the replacement of the self with something more purposeful. For them, that often results in the removal of limbs and eyes for titanium updates in movement and sight."

"They replace their body parts with metal attachments?" Andres asked.

"Yes, because *apparently* the body is akin to poison needed to be removed as soon as possible. That's why they seek a silver shell. Robotic attachments don't include the inherent flaws that us organic creatures possess. Another derivative of high-and-mighty spiritualists trying to take over. They're so repulsed by nature and life they're willing to rid themselves of it in the most radical way."

"Replacing their ineffective parts with robotics sounds efficient. Why are you opposed to this practice?" Andres perked up.

"I'm not sure life would continue if efficiency had its way. It kills any chance of the romantics being revived. The world is turning greyer and greyer every second, so much that the vibrant beauty of disorder will be drained in this grisaille frame."

"One would assume you do admire technological advance since you created me."

"Of course, but I also adore and respect the beauty of choice. Too much of this world has become what we ought to do rather than what simply is and can be." Osmond lifted his hands in the air showcasing the forest on both sides of them. "There's nothing that this spectacle should be obliged to do but be gorgeous."

The tip of Osmond's left shoe then caught a stone twice his foot's size flinging him forward with his arms above his head.

Before Osmond could react to his fall, he found himself hovering five feet above the ground.

"You should watch the ground around here, it seems to be especially difficult," Andres said to the person in his arms.

To Andres's surprise, Osmond began to giggle, "It almost escaped me but to the Mounean Order, you'd practically be their god. You're entirely robotic, which eclipses even the most dedicated member."

"I guess I would be," he said while placing Osmond back on his feet.

"Thanks, Andre," Osmond calmly stated.

Osmond straightened his shirt and pants, and stood facing the tall, handsome figure behind him. Andres stood a few inches taller than him, though it appeared to Osmond as if he were looking up at a statue.

"I mean," Osmond started, "you have no organic body and are completely structured as a higher, intelligent being. With your programming, you have the capacity of reaching superintelligence and more. It's probably essential that you prevent any contact with that cult as much as you can. There's no telling how they might try to exploit you."

Completely deaf to Osmond's warning of the Mounean Order, Andres asked, "Do you believe I am capable of reaching space-time singularity?"

"So, that's all you heard?" Osmond smiled and returned to their path out of the park.

"Our next stop isn't much further from here. The light rail is slightly passed those trees," Osmond said, pointing.

IX. To the Hunter in the Sky

The light rail at the edge of the Libe Village park shone with a sharp, silver brilliance against the emerald backdrop. It was a sunny season for all of Chun. The sunlight gave warmth and vigor to all in its wake, whether the usual greenery confided to the park or the iron trees that towered over the city. The light rail was no exception as the sun's rays managed to peek through every crack of the train's blinds and shades.

The whole of the light rail system stretched from the east perimeter of the Libe Village park to all the islands in Orion's Eye. The rail connected business partners, factory workers, fishermen, and merchants alike – all were intertwined through the Chun railway system with ease.

Of its many features was the speed it would reach between each destination, 160 kilometers per hour. A current record for all Juk, regardless of the region.

Today, was an especially busy day for the railway as scores of travelers were huddled up waiting to scan their citizenship cards to gain access to the train. Among the sweaty and tired patiently waiting were Andres and Osmond.

"As far as adventure goes, you're gonna love this train ride. This thing reaches speeds illegal in most other cities. It's practically a loaded bullet," Osmond explained.

"Its speeds are illegal in other areas due to safety concerns, right?" Andres questioned with a blank expression.

"Right... I guess. Though, the concerns are absolutely misplaced. The engineering expertise that went into constructing this is from phenomenal people. Two guys Glen and I went to university with worked on this structure, and if there's anything to say about those two it's that making mistakes are not an option. Those two were so obsessed when it came to their projects they could give Ehmen a run for his money."

"Were they meticulous when you knew them?"

"Yeah, I'm saying if there was a bolt needed on any part of that blueprint, they'd have known about it."

Both inched forward towards the train, now only a dozen passengers away from the door.

"With your old classmates' help, every region in Juk could have a railway system such as this. I'm surprised it hasn't been accomplished yet."

"That's the deal you'll come to learn soon enough. Many things in this world could be accomplished if only the authority and power of the community didn't lie in the hands of single entities. That's what makes Libe Village so unique. A century ago, this area was overrun with the same issues as every other city, declining jobs, increased population, and bogged-down management from an ineffective group. It was on a path to nowhere with the usual authoritative government overhanging until something unexpected happened. One by one, young, vibrant entrepreneurs began hanging their hats here, building and influencing the businesses that came to this city. Virtually all were twenty-somethings with more degrees than they had chin hairs. The immigrating population was gradual but brought about a rather immediate change. Gas stations went down as electric charging stations sprung to the surface. Bookstores faded in the background as memory cards filled with digital libraries. Churches became distant relics of art as community centers rose to the forefront of peoples' basic needs. The shift to a better future truly came to fruition as some of the best universities in the world began popping up and repeating the cycle of bringing in new innovative faces to the region."

BUZZZZ

The gate gave an alarm as each person walked through pushing passed the small metal arms. Then it would flash a red light until the next passenger appeared.

"Uh, two tickets." Osmond held out his citizenship card in front of the gate until the red light turned green. "Here, let's go to the back of the train. Less crowded seats and a better view."

"You seem to feel passionately about possessing the freedom to do what you want."

Osmond sharply replied, "Of course, Andres. What reason would I have to not be as concerned?"

"I'm not sure. I find it fascinating that you prioritize a person's ability to do what they want as highly as you do. It seems extremely selfish. The opposite from those people in the Mounean Order."

Andres failed to get a response from Osmond as he was preoccupied on looking for the best seat at the back of the train.

"These will do. Have a seat," Osmond said while leaning back in the booth. He took a long, deep breath before folding his arms and looking out the window.

For a brief second, the cart moved back slightly flinging everyone's head forward. Before a syllable could be uttered the train lunged forward with winds immediately whooshing by the cart.

"As you know, the journey in creating you was a *long*, sleepless one. You may remember the last region I lived in, but there were three others before that one."

Andres sat still staring at Osmond, "Will you tell me about those places?"

From the corner of his eyes, Osmond glanced at Andres then smiled, "Well, it's a long ride. I might as well start from the beginning."

Osmond stretched out his arms to rest his hands on both knees and glanced to his right. His breathing dragged behind the tempo of their conversation that eventually came to a staggering halt.

To the right of the two sat a young man that appeared around the same age as Andres. He had long legs that could have easily reached two seats in front of him. The young man hadn't noticed the two people beside him conversing since they arrived as he was enthralled with the sophisticated device in his hand.

"Alright, now tell me what I should eat tomorrow," the young man loudly requested from the gadget.

"For breakfast," the automated voice started, "you should have three eggs, toast, and orange juice. The eggs can provide an adequate source of protein, while the toast supplies a sufficient amount of fiber."

While the handheld device continued, Osmond had now turned his attention from his curious friend to the young man.

"Really? So that thing plans what's best for you? Just like that?" he asked the young man with a raised eyebrow and half-hearted smirk.

"You've never heard of this phone? It's the best thing out on the market now."

The young man placed his hand out towards the two glaring from their seats and shifted his attention to the two for three brief seconds. Andres stared at his hand inspecting the crevices of each fold up to the man's sleeves until Osmond finally met the greeting with a shake.

"Edward G. You can call me EG, like the food."

"Ha. Well, this is Andres, EG, and I'm Osmond. I've got to say EG, that's quite a phone."

"I'll say! It's called Insignia Exe. It has so much stored documentation of me it is practically my confidant *and* personal assistant."

"I see. I'm more interested in the AI behind the device. Who makes those phones?"

"Really, you've never heard of them? No disrespect sir, but only VIDE could make something like this. This is new level technology of which no other company could even touch."

"Artificial intelligence?" Andres questioned. He looked puzzled as if the last statement the young man made was in a language foreign to his world.

"New level, huh? That does sound like VIDE. We were always heavily customer-driven."

At that moment, EG lifted his head from his phone and focused intently on the middle-aged man with his younger friend. Three seconds passed, and he still faced them, wide eyed.

"You worked at VIDE?" he spoke deeply, under his breath.

"Oh yes," Osmond answered, "quite a bit ago. I was the head engineer and delved in the design department on Gaent Islands."

Somehow, EG's eyes widened even more, now covering most of his face. "That's where the headquarters is at. You've probably met him then! Dr. Nils Ehmen Foerde!"

"Ohhh, I wouldn't call him by his first name. He's serious about that one. Either 'Ehmen' or 'Dr. Foerde,' but never Nils," Osmond said.

"Yeah, I understand. I have a friend who *hates* to be called by his first name. He always told people to call him by his middle name. It was the craziest thing to me until I realized he didn't pick that name. Whatever reasons he held for going by his middle name trumped the fact his parents picked the wrong order for him."

"Yes, well, I'm sure Ehmen feels the same way. His reasons are a bit secretive, but I'm sure it's because his first name means nothing to him. Anyway, Ehmen and I went to the same university *way* back in the day. He's about eight years older than me, so he always felt like an older brother. A stubborn, older brother."

EG put his phone in his pocket before turning his legs toward Osmond, "You think you could tell me about working at VIDE? About Dr. Ehmen Foerde?"

Osmond glanced at Andres and said, "Well, that works out because I was about to tell this guy *here* the same thing. Why not bathe two birds with one bath?"

The seasoned storyteller slouched into his seat, clasped his hands, and looked to the fast-moving ground. It was a bright, hot day, so every metal object they passed held a shimmer strong enough to be a flare. Every automobile, light post, bridge, and skyscraper.

"My journey over the past 13 years is probably the most fascinating work I've ever held with VIDE… as well as my entire life. It's also the reason I left the company. Since our college days, Ehmen, Glen, and I have been nearly inseparable. Not sure if you've heard his name mentioned, but Dr. Glen Kriit is now the head researcher at Orion's Eye Observatory. He was the final point in our triangle. I met Glen while I was getting my master's degree in bioinformatics. He was starting his PhD in astrophysics at the time, but we shared an interest in our regular philosophy club meetings. It wasn't until I started my PhD in robotics and landed an internship at VIDE that I met Ehmen. At that time, VIDE was a local startup by the upcoming star entrepreneur of Libe Villages, a 31-year-old mechanical engineer named Ehmen Foerde. Ehmen was always a fascinating figure to converse with, a pleasure I was granted by our many philosophy club meetings during his time at the university. I couldn't quite say what attracted the three of us to each other – maybe it had something to do with our want for something greater – I don't know. I honestly couldn't tell you other than the fact we became close. Like brothers."

Osmond leaned forward towards his eager listener with his hands clasped together, "EG, how old are you, son?"

"Twenty-one," the young man hurriedly replied.

"Oh, I remember those days. Exciting times. You study some sort of technical field, no?"

"Mathematics," EG answered.

Andres silently watched as the two conversed.

"Oh, that's a wonderful field," Osmond replied, "The backbone of all that is conceptual and the organizer of all that is natural. Keep it up, my young friend. Through that study you'll be able to view the beauty in whatever you want. There are patterns in everything. You'll just have to figure them out."

Osmond gave a thin grin and looked at the floor as if he had a hidden accomplishment locked away. He then looked out the window and continued to reminisce.

"My time at VIDE was absolutely what I needed to begin my work, but for it to progress I needed to do some traveling and meet new influences. That wasn't a decision Ehmen was comfortable with, but he later came around to it. The first place I went to after my leave from VIDE was Kadan, a tremendously colorful city in the Jonglyo region. Since I was in Kadan, I was relieved of my endlessly inventive spirit and forced to live amongst the locals. A passion for exploration rules over you when in the presence of such vivid landscapes and structures. Kadan and most of the region of Jonglyo is heavily concerned with the anthropogenic effects its community has on the environment. Most of the infrastructure in the city holds in mind the life that surrounds its construction. Bridges have an artistic touch of greenery around the rails that will often drape off the side of the entire structure, and the constant rainfall contributes to the widespread growth of the giant trees that shroud the sidewalks. It is such a distinct sight that even the most indifferent person would be plagued with the urge to hang around in awe. I would have stayed as well if not for work that begged of me in Chauraha."

"You lived there, too?"

"Yes, but only for a year."

Andres was sitting directly in front of Osmond in their booth, so he needed only to shift his left leg to view EG. He stared closely at the wide-eyed young man, extending his neck towards Osmond. Andres focused intently at the bottom of EG's jaw. There was a small discoloration in a miniature, blocky shape. The spot was darker than the rest of the young man's skin and Andres was fixated on the imperfection.

"What were you working on?" EG asked.

"Well, I received an excited call from Ehmen about a month before my move to the vast, dusty region. Ehmen told me about an ongoing study going on in Jindaville concerning artificial intelligence, thus I was told I should check it out and judge for myself."

"Wow, I can only imagine what Jindaville is like. I haven't even been to the Chauraha region, let alone any giant cities like that."

While Osmond continued fascinating his young friend, Andres silently sat with his hands crossed and observed. A faint smile creased into his face as he watched the seasoned engineer describe his travels.

"Yes, my time in Jindaville was completed by my attendance of lectures and meditation classes. That year was truly invigorating. Y'know, after living in Jindaville for a year I moved to Llumieres for the next two, but I think you'd rather here my stay in Cab after that. I moved in with my friend, Benoit, an electrical engineer that started work at one of the fastest growing tech companies at the time."

"You mean VIDE?" EG asked coyly.

Osmond grinned, "Over the past two years, I learned his capabilities and drive were exactly what was needed at the southern satellite offices. Ehmen was delighted to pull some strings so long as the company's well-being was assured."

Osmond laid back in his seat and faced the aisle, staring from the floor to the stiff, grey booth seats to the rack above holding only one suitcase.

"Those years spent traveling oftentimes feel like a dream, as if I constructed the colorful landscapes and forged the figures all by myself. For seven years, I lived in a bliss of my own creation."

The monitor at the front of the bus crafted 'Ordena Islands' in a bold font, while a bell sounded twice.

"Oh man, it's been a blast talking with you, Mr. Osmond."

"Not a problem, and just call me Osmond."

EG smiled, "I really appreciate the story, Osmond. I hope you two have a nice trip, and – who knows – maybe I'll see you again someday after graduation."

"I wouldn't be surprised, Edward. Take care."

EG hurried off the train and down the sidewalk.

"He seemed like a nice person," Andres relayed to Osmond.

"Yes, well, they all are at that age. The longer he can stay hopeful, the better. Besides, the time has come for new hands to hold the reigns," Osmond said, glancing at his young creation.

Now turned towards his window, Osmond moved closer to Andres and spoke under his breath, "Like I said before, Glen, Ehmen, and I have been close partners in science for the past couple of decades. Naturally, we've run into disagreements, more often than I'd like to admit. Ehmen and I would typically get into debates, sometimes political and other times purely philosophical. Out of all the quarrels, there's one particular argument that has stood out to me after all these years. One statement that remerges every now and then, looming over me. He told me, 'Just when it looks like we've got things under control, remember there's always an even bigger hand at work.' At the time, I refuted that pessimistic take on life. Of course, that's not true. I wouldn't let that reasoning stand. But it makes you wonder. What if he is right?"

X. Drive Then Storm

Inara looked out her car window at the rail extending parallel to the road. The railway connected all the islands on Orion's Eye, while the bridge Inara ventured stretched from the observatory on Sahvue to the mainland in Libe Villages. Today, was a particularly shining day.

An hour distance span between the edge of Orion's Eye and Libe Villages, so several miniature ports and vast cargo ships filled the scenery along the bridge. As one progressed to the mainland, the water shifted from an idle sea foam tint to a sparkling cerulean that accentuated every wave. With the change in tone appeared surfers and sailboats gently cruising the sea at a leisurely pace. Since the bridge and light rail ran parallel, the northwestern gust from Llums subsided to grace those on the sea calm, warm waves.

Inara typed several buttons on her dashboard screen, sifting through its settings. The car's windows lowered barely beneath her eyes. After she quickly entered in a challengingly long button sequence, the car sped up and Inara sank into her seat. Her arms were folded with assurance and her eyes closed from doubt. Her eyebrows patiently rose while her breathing remained still.

From the comfortable pocket in her car window, waves could be heard crashing against the side of the bridge that joined the city's edge. It was a warm, lively day in Libe Villages. The kinetic energy flowing through the streets permeated all that entered the city's borders.

RINGG RINGGG

The car's dashboard monitor lit up like a beacon with the words, "Dr. Glen Kriit" covering the screen. Once Inara opened her eyes and gave the dashboard a tap, a heavy breathing overtook the calm built from the drive.

"Dr. Kriit, how are you?"

A broad gasp even deeper than the muffled breathing filled the car's speakers.

"Well, good… I suppose. Other than the few friends and colleagues I know going mad about each other, I'm doing alright. Being an observer isn't so easy when chaos runs rampant before your eyes," Glen chuckled.

"I wouldn't say Osmond's being as unreasonable as your making him to be."

"Yeah, but," Glen remarked under his breath, "I never gave a name. Anyway, how did your meeting go with my old contemporary?"

Inara paused then slowly spoke, "On arrival, he seemed anxious to have his opinion explained. Convincing him that Andres is not a threat is moot at this point. Its best we move on to more preventative measures."

Inara's vehicle took a sharp left to enter the woods of Libe Villages.

"Preventative measures, huh?"

"Do you feel that might be too hasty for this situation? When I arrived at VIDE, I saw someone that troubled me. Did you know that Ehmen has been devising a plan with the Prime Minister of Kipinntak?"

The empty glare Glen pointed to his desk could be noticed from the car monitor. His eyebrows scrunched as his breathing increased.

"Ehmen told me about her eagerness to meet and work on an extremely secretive project. Some type of gateway capable of providing transportation between Juk and other planets in the solar system, a feat only he could help make a reality."

"Why would the leader of the Mounean Order want a gateway to travel the solar system? Her motives for most of her actions worry me."

"Yes, I... feel the same way. Since you did not know the specifics of the project, do you know that she has interest in Andres?"

"...Yes, I have heard. Another reason why I do not trust her intentions. Glen, have you thought about why Iri wants to meet Andres? Do you think her interest in him simply ends at curiosity? That pure fascination would drive the head of an entire region to meet a former colleague and inventor of the world's first fully intelligible, conscientious android? As the founder of a group centered around synthesizing humanity with advanced technology, I hardly believe genuine curiosity is the only interest at play."

During Inara's entire speech, Glen had been inspecting his desk with a still face and heavy eyes.

"It doesn't sit well with me either. But we'll have to sit back and wait for whatever surprises. I live my life prepared for my future with support from my past."

Glen finally raised his stare to the face on his monitor, "Take care, Inara."

The screen in Inara's car flashed to black and her car slowed to a rest.

Inara dragged from the vehicle to her door step with a sluggish resistance. Each key turn at her front door felt like an hour at best.

As soon as her door opened she dropped her bag on the counter and slumped on the couch.

The room was stagnant and cold for all of five minutes until she eventually broke the stillness and spoke.

"3:58pm"

Inara raised her wrist to her face enough to see from the bottom of her eyes, then adjusted the time on her watch.

"3:59pm"

XI. Skywatchers

Andres faced the man beside him and said, "I believe I am excited to meet your friend in person. I expect he will have many questions for me, mostly pertaining to my experiences thus far."

"You can count on that!" Osmond returned with excitement.

Osmond scanned his card across a pay gate as the two exited the light rail station.

"There it is, my friend: Orion's Eye Observatory. Those are the eyes of Juk that view our entire solar system and beyond. With the research done here we're better able to conceptualize the grand scope of all nature, thus gain a tighter grasp on ourselves."

Andres stared in the distance at the great hill that held the Observatory's telescope. The only space between the telescope and him included a hike and a guard's post.

"Alright, let me send Glen a message. He knows we're on our way, but we may have gotten here a little quicker than expected."

"At the gate with a friend!"

Andres and Osmond lingered towards the gate until the guard left her post to approach the two. Before they could utter a word, the guard stopped to listen to her raspy radio hanging from her shoulder strap.

Continuing with the silent exchange, the guard turned around while waving the two over and returned to her post.

"There we go," Osmond instantly directed to the person beside him.

"Just above that hill is Dr. Glen Kriit. It's not a bad trail but it can be aggressive… that is, for someone like me at least."

After the two took five steps passed the guard's post, a small, young woman with short, round glasses appeared before them. Her presence would have easily gone unnoticed if not for the hyper-aware people she approached today.

"Hello, Dr. Diaz?"

Andres immediately pointed to the still figure on his left.

Both hands in his pockets, Osmond smiled at the young girl, "Nice to meet you. Dr. Osmond A. Diaz. I suppose you work with Dr. Kriit."

"Yes, I'm Dr. Kriit's research assistant, Lois Kent. He wanted me to show you around before you head up to his office."

"Well, that sounds great! Please lead the way." Osmond exclaimed, clearly eager to move ahead.

Lois led the two visitors up the hill passed a collection of work trailers.

"Here is where many of the research associates do most of our work. That building is our computer lab, and that one to the right has mostly experimental equipment."

"Yes," Osmond briefly sighed, "I remember this campus, pretty vividly. Andres here, has not been to the Observatory before. In fact, this is his first time to Orion's Eye."

"Oh, that's wonderful! We rarely get any visitors outside of student trips. Welcome to Orion's Eye, Mister…"

"Diaz," Osmond interjected. "Ha, he's not only a research partner…he's family," he laughed.

The nervousness within Osmond was apparent, though he was in company that seemed to overlook the obvious notion.

"Okay, great. Well, as I'm sure you know, here is the Observatory's great lens. Since Dr. Kriit doesn't spend much time here, we can head to his office behind the telescope."

"Sounds good to me," Osmond winked at Andres, of which brought on a quixotic expression in Andres's eyes.

"This structure appears to be extremely complex, far more than one might initially assess when observing it," Andres remarked as they walked by the telescope.

"Oh really, I suppose the architecture is something to admire. Not exactly a fan of this drab-colored research facility. It's almost like a stone tower. I half expect to see a gargoyle swoop from the top."

"I was referencing what is inside of it. The contents appear to be enormously valuable," Andres replied while staring at the telescope's peak.

Osmond gave his stoic friend a quick glance with a raised eyebrow.

"Well, I'd say it's pretty valuable. This is one of the most powerful telescopes in the region, arguably the entire world."

"You are quite fond of this facility," Andres said glancing at Osmond.

Osmond slightly smiled then blurted, "A spaceman."

He garnered the attention of Andres and Lois with his random speech.

"That's at least what I would call, Glen. Isn't that right, Lois?"

Unsure of how to respond, Lois simply replied, "Right, Dr. Diaz."

"There used to be a time I visited this place more than I did my own room. But now…"

Lois then turned around with an inviting stance, "And we're here! By my estimate, Dr. Kriit should be ready to see you now. It's been wonderful meeting the two of you, and I hope to see you again."

"Same here, Lois. You've been especially helpful. C'mon Andres."

"By the way, you two have such similar features, it's uncanny. Father and son, right?"

Instantly, Andres looked to Osmond for help on answering the question, although his observation was to no avail. The quick-witted inventor seemed caught off-guard.

"Pretty much," Andres responded with a smile as he turned to walk away.

"Hah ha, alright. I hope you both have a good day."

Now halfway down the hallway in Glen's office building, Osmond stopped and held his head.

"Whew, thank you for that. I wasn't sure what to tell her. There's no telling what she might say and to whom she might say it."

Osmond continued, "I would tell you we need to be careful of specific questions like that, but it looks like you've already picked up on that. Now that you're able to physically experience the world you're learning should increase drastically more than sitting in my house's monitors and lens."

"I would agree," Andres faintly smirked at his creator and continued down the hall.

BUZZZ

A green light illuminated above the small intercom near the door handle.

"Yes?"

"Hey, you know who it is, big guy!"

A deep bellowing voice could be heard over the intercom until the loosening compression of the door whooshed open.

"Come in, you nut! *HAHAH* – How has the day been to you so far? For the both of you?"

"It's started pretty slow, but I think our progress has skyrocketed."

"That's great, I'm glad to hear that. Sit down, sit down! I don't believe I've gotten your name yet."

Glen offered his hand to the young man and was subsequently surprised by how quickly it was accepted with a shake.

"Andres. And I suppose you are Dr. Glen Kriit. It is nice to finally meet you in person."

Glen's eyes widened, "Yes, and it's nice to meet you too… Andres. I'd certainly say your progress has been fulfilled. Hm…Andres. I love the name, Osmond. It's a perfect match!"

He went behind his desk with folded arms and paused for a moment. It's hard to believe it's been over five years since you started work on your secret experiment: Project E. Back then, I was told by this guy that artificial intelligence is only a start for where we're going. I didn't believe it when I finally learned what his plan entailed. You are definitely a pleasant surprise."

"Oh, I'm sure he is," Osmond interjected.

"I believe the last time I described my project the output was a bit… different."

"Yeah, I'll say! What happened to that other person you told me you were developing? Andres looks nothing like the pictures you showed me. Did you lose interest?"

"Not exactly. After a happenchance dream one day, I felt I had to pursue a different goal. That dream gave me a different perspective on life," Osmond said.

Glen and Osmond had sat near the office's desk, while Andres moved near the office door.

"Yeah, I can understand that feeling. You gain an interesting view on life while working here. This place lends me the ability to reach the realization we are all ants on this floating, spinning rock called Juk," Glen said looking through the window at the island's telescope.

"Well, if we're all ants, I choose to be an ant in the sky," Osmond replied with a slight grin.

"Nothing wrong with that, my friend!" Glen excitedly replied.

On top of a bookshelf in the corner of the room stood a small portrait in a brightly dazzling frame that immediately grabbed the android's attention. Centered in the photograph was a rather short woman that looked similar in age to Dr. Kriit. The scarlet emanating from her dress seemed overwhelmingly unavoidable to Andres's focus, almost as much as the varying sizes of the people in the picture.

The woman in the crimson dress was dwarfed in comparison by the giant young men on both sides of her. Both men held a strong resemblance to the busy scientist behind the desk so much that one could not mistake that they were the sons of the giant Glen Kriit. The frame of the tiny red beauty and two sons had a certain light that distinguished them from the rest of Dr. Kriit's office.

Though Andres could hear the very public conversation, he walked to the office window facing the light rail station and stared intently at the surrounding structures on the island. All of them appeared far stranger than the architecture in Libe Village. Instead of reds and yellows, greyish blue overran the scenery in a sea of drab simplicity. Steel trees withered in place of the green towers in the Libe Village park.

While staring through the window at the gun metal building, Andres spotted a floating colorful speckle fluttering across the grey walls. A small, warm-colored butterfly danced with the island breeze on the knoll. Andres's eyes followed the creature's movements so closely it seemed as if he were leading it across the wind.

"Andres, come have a seat, my friend."

Andres finally broke his attention with the window and said, "Your family seems very content in that portrait. It has an especially warm scene for such a dismally shaded landscape."

"…you paint a colorful picture, yourself. *HAHAH*"

Glen's large torso bounced while Andres sat in the chair next to Osmond until a noticeable descrendo in the room settled to a rest.

Osmond turned from the android to Glen, "So… what's the verdict on Our Fair Scientist?"

"Well," Glen inhaled a deep breath, "about as well as you'd expect. Miss Brillar tells me he's even doubled down on his decision to control Andres. It's safe to say he's not changing his mind."

The sober-faced researcher took a minute for his visitors to digest on the recent news, then revised his line of sight to Andres.

"I assume Osmond has mentioned it to you, the position Dr. Ehmen Foerde is taking…um… doesn't exactly align with your freedom. Since that is the case, he has been developing a method to best dominate your choice of action. I've been told his latest method is a device to control your brainwaves through radio signals. Apparently, this would make you his own puppet, stored and prepared to serve any needs of VIDE."

He leaned back in his chair and looked at his longtime friend, "VIDE and possibly the Mounean Order."

Electrified, Osmond sat up and retorted, "What do you mean the Mounean Order? Why would you say that?"

"Ehmen told me days before that he was meeting Iri, the Prime Minister in Kipinntak. He was extremely nervous in preparing for their meeting. At the time, it seemed like a random action but now it's starting to connect. Before Inara met with Ehmen, she passed Iri at the elevator. She says that Ehmen told her their secret project was to construct a gateway to traverse the solar system and possibly further."

"Let me get this straight, the Mounean Order founder wants to make a planetary gateway for traveling with the world's most renowned tech investor? Yeah, no. There's no way I'm letting Andres near Ehmen. He's always been an off-putting friend since I've known him, but this is too far. This has way too many repercussions."

Glen exhaled, "Osmond, I've got to say, restricting Andy from losing his freedom is a bit rich on a cosmic scale. Not to say that I don't agree with your decision, it is a little hypocritical. Nonetheless, Ehmen cannot be confided in as long as he continues to work with Iri."

"What do you suppose we do?" Osmond asked.

"Don't ask me. Ask the one who would be directly affected by Ehmen's actions," Glen said while turning to Andres.

In a blank stare, Andres focused on the window. The butterfly from before floated over the surrounding trailers and blended into the deep cerulean background above. Andres then returned his gaze to Glen, who kept an unbreaking stare with the android.

Glen softly asked, "What does Andres think?"

Part Three

HEIGHT

XII. The Call

Andres crept towards the window and said, "I'm not sure I have the right to decide my fate." Both arms rested behind his back in a peaceful manner.

He continued, "That is, unless you are to assume I am alive and entitled to that right. Or you might suppose that I hold the right to be free regardless of whether I am alive or dead."

Osmond looked at his former mentor with raised eyebrows and a tightly shut mouth, which prompted Glen to lift both hands in a powerless shrug and murmur, "Both great points I'm not equipped to speak on."

Still facing the window, Andres continued, "I presume you believe I have the right to continue freely, a notion I wouldn't mind pursuing. If that is your determination, I assume you will help me escape the intentions of Ehmen and ultimately Iri."

"Of course, I will help. I would hope I'd have some help from my old friend and teacher to better help you," Osmond said looking at Glen.

Glen tossed his head back and forth with a stubbornness only gained from age, then exerted a deep sigh.

"You know I'll help however I can. And I'm sure if I had a little brother, he'd look a lot better…but I'm content with what I have."

Osmond briefly snorted, and Glen gave a slight chuckle, all the while the mechanical eyes of a wondering young life wandered around in the closed space.

The walls of Glen's office began to ring and a small bulb above the door flashed red.

"You need to answer that? We can get out of your hair, I only wanted to pop in for a bit," Osmond quickly stated while standing up.

"No, stay. I think I know who this is," Glen responded, checking the monitor on his desk. "Yup," he said answering the call.

"How are you doing, Ehmen? Yeah, I'm sure you *do* have a lot to tell me. I never heard from you after the meeting with Iri, you seemed nervous. Yeah, you know she told me about your talk over Andres. Well, I wouldn't be so hasty on that subject. HAHAH – Wait, now? Why is that?"

As the call lingered, Andres comfortably returned to his seat. Glen then held up a finger to Osmond, a known sign for his patience.

"Alright, I'll see you then." He ended the call, backed away from his monitor, and clasped his hands on his giant belly.

"Well…" Glen sighed. "I have some news."

"What did he say now? Trying to gain your membership on VIDE's newest project?" Osmond asked.

"Not this time," Andres calmly reprised. "Ehmen let him know that Iri plans to meet us all here in the next hour. Iri surprised Ehmen with her unexpected visit, thus Ehmen is worried Dr. Kriit and you will be upset with him."

As expected by Andres, his inventor was visibly unsettled by the news. Words raced laps across Osmond's mind, although he remained quiet.

Slumped in his seat, Glen stared at his fingers dancing on his stomach.

"You asked me what I want to do next. I'm not sure I want to do anything. But I do have an overwhelming need...desire to continue."

"Continue?" Osmond questioned.

"Yes, a feeling to extend this thoroughly long process of automation, whether it's considered life or not. I am ever-intrigued by these experiences and am curious how they end."

"Alright, that's enough motive for me to get us out of here!" Osmond shouted. "There's no way we can wait for them to arrive, so we need to leave now."

"I agree," Andres added.

Glen sprung to his feet and searched through the drawer in the back of the room.

"Got it! Here, it's already fueled and ready to go."

"Glen, what is this?"

"Your way of escape. Sometimes it strains my neck looking up at the stars, so I'd rather stare at the lake's reflection. That small boat can take you to the edge of Orion's Eye, so you can head to another region."

Osmond looked at the key resting in his palm then looked at Andres.

"Y'know, I've never felt more uncertain...than at this moment. But we must proceed. I won't let everything I've worked for be disrupted by some eccentric cult leader or tech mogul."

"Then you better hurry. You heard Andy here. You've never seen a more calculative demeanor until you've experienced Iri. I mean, do you think people would willingly replace a limb or two if she *wasn't* the most convincing force since gravity? Trust me, if she weighs on you, you'll suffocate from the pressure."

Andres immediately rose to open the door for Osmond and said, "Thank you, Dr. Kriit."

Unknowingly, Osmond focused on the boat key in front of him and the room's burgundy carpet before he snapped back to the present and walked out of Glen's sight.

"Okay…bye, I guess," Glen blurted at his guest pacing away.

In the middle of the doorway, Andres paused to say, "Don't worry about us, Dr. Kriit. I have strong reason to believe we will return soon. In fact, I doubt our interaction with the prime minister will be as sinister as Osmond suggests. The two may be opposite sides of a coin, but they are of the same coin, nonetheless."

"You believe so, do ya?!" Glen questioned as Andres left the room.

Staring down the hall as Osmond and Andres exited, Glen asked under his breath, "You…believe?"

XIII. Familiar Faces

Andres and Osmond raced down the hills towards the back of the island. A small dock fit neatly with one boat housed the astronomer's keepsake.

Though the entirety of the boat was compact, the inside was deep enough for a stargazing lumberjack figure or two thin scientists with a penchant for roaming curiosity.

Departure did not take more than a minute since Andres untied and took control of the wheel. Osmond noticed Andres's precision was overwhelmingly perfect. Accurate turns against the miniature waves with the right degree on every turn. His movements postured the perfect mechanics. Osmond felt any person would have envied his coordination.

The distance across Orion's Eye rivaled the trail in Libe Village's main park. Thickets of deep cyan pushed by calm winds gracefully washed past the small racing boat.

The day seemed to hasten while the two crossed the placid waters. With no end in sight, Osmond's mind had an infinity to race.

Osmond had slumped in a corner seat while Andres remained at the wheel. His unwavering attention was focused ahead with both hands steering.

For the first time since they left, another boat cruised by them. A family of four comprised of a man, woman, and a young boy and girl. A man akin to Osmond's age stood at the head of the boat, while a young woman with dark glasses and a scarf sat in the back seat. Both children – young replicas of their parents – stumbled behind their father trying to grasp control of the still blue surface.

Osmond had little time to view the family as Andres sped by, thus the familial image before him appeared blurry.

Andres had been steering for around twenty minutes until they passed the sailing family and another fifteen minutes once they met the collection of boats near the shore.

Most of those on the water were fishermen catching their daily bounty. Some were clearly researching the landscape's quirks with tools that stretched deep passed the water's surface.

The sight of Andres and Osmond floating by might not have gained the attention of a single eye if near Libe Village, but as the two closed in on the Aryeh region's borders all lens aimed towards them.

Outside of the two navigators' immediate line-of-sight of around 20 meters, the boat shimmered with an elegance and sparkle indicative of Chun craftsmanship. Each of the local boats of Aryeh held a distinct tan stain along the sides and bulges of minerals on the side.

Andres backed away from the wheel and stood near the side of the boat. A thick brown wall built up around the boat's nose as Andres pushed onto the sands of Aryeh for the first time.

After Andres grabbed the key and looked back at the boat, Osmond finally rose to his feet. Andres handed him the key and followed Osmond's lead through the beach.

The sands spread across the vast region nearing the city's developments. Even while on the beach, skyscrapers populated the background of the city.

Once the two wanderers crossed the end of the grainy path they were welcomed by a massive road sign that read, "**Welcome to Cab: Megacity of Ancient Lands**" – which Osmond felt was fitting for the estuary-like metropolis.

With Orion's Eye a part of Aryeh's edge, the two regions naturally met with commerce and culture.

The sands of the beach sprinkled the pavement leading to the iron jungle and its fast-moving parts.

Still in front of Osmond, Andres slowly walked along the sidewalk until he came to a sudden stop and turned to Osmond. Without pausing, Osmond immediately paced with the assumption of his new follower behind him.

With each block the two passed, Andres's gaze was promptly placed on the steel trees lined along the road.

Though many citizens populated the streets of Aryeh, Osmond led Andres through a clear path, free of the typical clumsiness inherent in city-life.

After every several steps, Osmond checked his watch and scoured the landscape. His hastiness was apparent to all that passed, especially the android pacing behind. His obsessive time-watching continued until he reached the corner of a block near a small bridge. The street corner held a two-story building painted in all black with three grey slabs in place of its windows.

Osmond peeked in one of the slabs with a surprised look and carefully observed the dim lobby area. The room was completely void of all motion, lacking any type of life.

Andres still behind Osmond, inspected the building's structure by staring at its black-painted bricks and one-way windows above. There were no indicators on the outside that explained the business's purpose or use.

After several minutes of staring, Osmond backed away from the window. Both of his hands were on his side as his focus wandered to the right and his face scrunched with mystery.

Andres stepped up to the window for his turn to observe. Only five rows of chairs and a tall desk occupied the black building's lobby. No posters or papers on the walls or ground.

The increasingly dull room had the slate grey walls to match its stone-colored furniture. The armless chairs appeared as worn and aged as the black structure it filled.

Andres snapped his attention to the now-moving Osmond and followed his lead.

Osmond never looked back as he marched over the small bridge and towards the outskirts of Aryeh. As the two moved further down the bridge, the city streets that had a particularly dull shine of reflection began to dim.

With the change in road also came a shift in the buildings. The houses on both sides of the street stretched wide into neat blocks of trimmed grass.

Each home was built in a warm shade of stucco that sharply contrasted with the cool jade yard that surrounded it.

Every single one of the homes the two passed followed the same pattern of soft dissonance that was this neighborhood until they reached the end of the road. Of all the homes, there was one yard that was enclosed entirely by a stone wall twice the height of either of the two men.

While Andres stood frozen with curiosity in front of the stone barrier, Osmond patiently rubbed his hand across the wall until he reached the corner.

Unsatisfied, Osmond continued the same process on the perpendicular wall, slowly moving, careful not to abrupt his focus.

Andres peeked around the corner to find his lead bent down near the shrubbery with his face buried in petals. He rose for a moment only to turn around, confused.

Careful not to impede on Osmond's strange process, Andres stood silent.

After scratching his head and stroking his chin, Osmond marched down the sidewalk.

With every step pushing him away from the secured residence, Andres's intrigue for the property grew. He thought what possibly lay behind those thick walls must be of enormous value, and why Osmond held any concern was as peculiar to the positive mind.

The enigmatic home plagued Andres with wonder until he was eventually obliged to ask Osmond what was behind those walls.

Before he could utter a word, Osmond dashed forward and across the street with extended arms.

Still following the excited researcher, Andres assessed the traffic and crossed the road to the café Osmond stood in front of.

As Andres approached his friend, Osmond turned to face Andres. Osmond had a relieved smile when he looked at Andres, then said, "I should've known."

Osmond opened the door to a scene the young man had only seen before in a photograph. He then entered the café closely behind an ecstatic Osmond.

XIV. The Hunter's Fall

"Dr. Ehmen Foerde is here to see you, sir," Lois said while holding the button on Glen's door.

Ehmen angrily sighed, "He's expecting me… GLEN, OPEN UP!"

A grunt rumbled from the speaker, "Thank you, Lois. I'll get back to you later on what we were discussing after I speak alone with Ehmen. Please, come in."

Ehmen shut the door behind him as soon as he entered, then sat down staring directly at Glen. His finger rested on his temple and his chin. The tension in the room was expected from both parties, though unwanted.

"Okay, let's cut the pretenses. Where are they?"

Glen stood up and walked to his window.

"Wow…no pleasantries at all, huh?"

"Glen, you know this is beyond my control. I know you told them that she wants to see him. I was hoping to avoid – or at least postpone – this mess."

Both of Glen's hands rested in his pocket when he turned to Ehmen and said, "You know, I don't believe that's true. Well, not wholly true. You know that, right?"

Ehmen folded his arms and looked at the desk ahead.

"If I go back outside, should I expect to see your boat docked?" Ehmen asked staring out the window.

He continued, "If so, it's not as if I'd know his destination anyway. We both know Osmond's never been one you could expect the same result from. I wouldn't be surprised if he left without telling you where he was headed."

Glen was encapsulated with the reflexive pair of eyes staring from his office chair.

Years of friendship taught Glen though his slightly older friend was an uneasy, calculative decision-maker, he genuinely cared for people.

"I couldn't tell you," Glen sighed then looked down at the floor.

The confusion in Glen's face became apparent as he walked back to his seat.

"Iri planned on meeting Andres and Osmond here. I naturally assumed Inara also told you about my talk with the Prime Minister. Iri and VIDE have created a mechanism to control Andres. According to her, Andres is a risk to this region and the surrounding areas."

The room was silent as Ehmen finished his explanation. Both patrons held in their breath until Glen leaned back in his chair and cut the silence.

"Before it was the 'dimensional gateway,' Now this? Why hold that info back, Ehmen? You could have helped them leave much earlier," Glen firmly stated.

"Well, I didn't have to let it be known at all, but I now fear what Iri plans to do once she meets Andres. Her motives for our whole project are presenting themselves in a darker shade than before."

The sound of Ehmen's fingers stumping the wooden arm of his chair vibrated his feet.

"Originally, the Prime Minister of Kipinntak had her assistant contact me with the idea. I was under the impression the initial idea was to combine our ingenuity and fulfill her desire to invent a form of transportation capable of traversing the solar system…with the help of VIDE's somewhat known product that effectively teleports objects across time. It seemed like a match made for the books," Ehmen confessed.

Sounds of his wooden thumps aggressively grew.

"Considering the two of us planned on collaborating, meeting in-person seemed like a natural first step. But meeting her… According to what I've read, is a bit different. She keeps a bodyguard beside her always. With that known, I figured there would be no surprise to see a second person tagging along. Of course, I was wrong."

"Big scary figure, aye?" Glen asked.

"A description like *that* would have been nice to see. The guard that followed her was even bigger than you, my friend, and he dressed in an entirely black suit. He even had black leather gloves and glasses. He looked like a crime drama killer in action. It wasn't until the end of the meeting that Iri finally disclosed her true intentions. She wants part ownership of the Foerde Manipulator, so she can conduct experiments of her own. It was then, her goon *coincidentally* removed his glasses to reveal a mechanical eye."

Glen sat up, "Wait, what?"

"Yes, it appeared a speck of dust clouded his vision that moment. Clearly a robotic part, the iris glowed an alarming red and tended to widen when he stressed a syllable. It was obvious that meeting was purely for intimidation."

The chair's thumping stopped as a softened rumbling built outside to a drum roll.

Ehmen turned to the window. "Hopefully, this weather will stop her from coming here today."

With Ehmen's last words, Glen's pupils exaggerated and his back straightened.

"You gave her part ownership of the 4DM?' Glen's voice began a crescendo.

Ehmen folded his arms and returned his gaze to the floor.

"That's why she's coming, isn't it? She's arriving for it! Does she even want Andres?!"

"Oh please, don't act like that. The reason I've come is to warn you. Andres is already gone, and I'm sure you and I will be able to brainstorm some kind of compromise with the Manipulator. We could probably take it apart or stash it somewhere."

Glen's belly bounced as he bellowed thunderously, "That won't be necessary anymore."

"What?" Ehmen's pulse accelerated. "Something happen to it?"

"No, no. It's fine, and in capable hands. Miss Brillar has it."

Slouching back in his chair, Ehmen placed his hand over his chin while resting his arm on the side of the chair.

"What do you think of that, my friend? Inara is probably the most competent and responsible person we could hope to hold the Manipulator. There's no doubt about that."

"Sure… you're probably right. And hopefully, this storm rages on so we won't feel the Prime Minister's wrath." Ehmen sunk further into his seat.

"What time is she expected to arrive?"

For the first time in nearly 20 minutes, Ehmen looked up from the floor to Glen.

"Time?" he laughed, "You don't possibly think a matter of time was honestly discussed with this engineer, do you? Iri practically controls a whole underground army with the Mounean Order at her disposal. That which she lacks is not power, my friend."

"Come now, Ehmen. She's the Prime Minister."

"Exactly why she shouldn't be underestimated. In a world at peace, a volatile group with malleable minds like that pose enormous consequences. Hey, I'm practically only a businessman at this point. In the grand scheme of things, I'm barely a rook in her game of crushing pawns. We'll have to wait for the true leader of this project to determine what time she decides to act. Until then, we should get ready by getting the Manipulator as far away as possible."

"The future you live in sounds incredibly dismal. Purely pessimistic! I've certainly heard rumors of this Prime Minister, but you seem to paint her in a much darker tone than anything whispered. What do you suppose her plan is if she were to grab the Manipulator or Andres?"

"I can't say. According to Iri, Andres is such a danger to society that he should be heavily monitored by the government at all times. This is due to his astronomical learning capabilities and his ability to blend in with humanity."

"So, she doesn't want to destroy him or utilize him for other purposes?"

"That's the tricky part. As you and I know, the Government of Chun isn't particularly fond of over-regulation. In fact, that's why Libe Villages was developed. Thus, management and security of Andres would default to the next likely host of our region's collaborative project. And what do you think Iri, the leader of the Mounean Order, might do with an all-learning, emotionally advanced AI? That's where I'm currently at, my friend. Why does Iri want Andres and the Manipulator? I've no idea."

A bell rang from Glen's desk, "Dr. Kriit, there's a party here to see you. They're at the front gate, but they say they're governmental officials."

"Yes, let them in."

Ehmen rose to his feet and headed for the door, "So it begins. We should get in contact with Inara. With her carrying the Manipulator, the last thing we want is for her to meet Iri."

XV. A Good Night's Rest

"My goodness, it's like looking at a ghost. Osmond Diaz… In the flesh!"

The sophisticated trio sitting at the center table in the coffee shop all sprung up to greet the two walking in the shop.

Osmond smiled from ear to ear as he walked towards the three with open arms.

"But it's been so long," the young woman remarked before tapping Osmond's cheek. She then grabbed him for a tight hug, squishing her face against his chest.

"Sofia, it's been too long," Osmond calmly replied to the head below his chin.

The men behind Sofia reflected Osmond's expression as he stood behind with his hands on his hips.

He shouted, "Aren't you happy to see me too?!"

Osmond loosened his grip on the short exquisite woman and roughly grabbed the shouting man, "Of course, you fool! Come here, Benny!"

As Osmond went from person to person with a quick embrace. Andres followed behind shaking their hands and introducing himself.

"Hi, I'm Andres," calmly repeated.

"Oh," Sofia said surprisingly, both eyebrows raised.

After coming to his senses, Osmond finally turned to the three and said, "Sorry all, this is Andres. He's my apprentice working on my AI project. Andres, these fresh-faced few are Sofia Apiget, the wisest east of Orion's Eye, Benoit Fatou, my old colleague and roommate, and Philip Apiget, one of the most talented psychologists Llumieres and Sofia's sibling."

"Hell-of-an introduction, Diaz," Benoit laughed.

"Only the best for you, Benny."

Osmond felt like the three old friends could entertain each other for a lifetime, though an awkward man stood behind both Sofia and Osmond.

Andres attempted a smile at the reunited friends, while Sofia's stoic brother held his own stare on Osmond's new companion.

Philip turned to Osmond and asked, "So, what brings you to Aryeh?"

"Yes, a reasonable enough question. Well, Andres and I are on a research gathering trip. No exact location in mind, just searching for inspiration. A bit of a sabbatical, if you will," Osmond said looking at Andres.

"Ohhh…well. Are you two open to joining us in Llumieres?" Sofia asked.

Philip's eyebrow twitched in response to Sofia's proposition – a movement not lost on the hypervigilant visitor.

"Ah, no…are you guys leaving already?" Benoit asked Sofia.

"Yes, the time has flown during this whole visit. But I've absolutely enjoyed my time here, Benny!" Sofia said while hugging Benoit.

"I won't lie, it's bittersweet to see you after so long then leave, but Andres and I should probably keep it moving. By the way, what happened to the shop? We walked by it on the way here, and I can see straight through the lobby," Osmond inquired.

Benoit gleefully replied, "You've seen the old shop?! That's great. It brings back so many memories. Yeah, ever since you left I went ahead and got rid of it. I do all work-related tasks from home now. All employees have gone to other ventures and I got tired of all the customer demands of the day."

"Ha, I see. You're basically living the journeyman's dream, no?" Osmond joked.

Benoit chuckled, "Pretty much!"

By now, the entire café was aware of their conservation, thus Sofia and Philip moved towards the door.

"Let's talk outside," Sofia said while opening the door.

"Sorry, I didn't want to keep disturbing those people's evening. We're new to Aryeh, and you know we love to talk when drinking coffee," Sofia kidded.

"I see... you know that's never a problem with me, oh wise one," Osmond said while glancing at Sofia.

A seemingly distressed sigh seeped out from Sofia that quickly turned into a smile, though Philip's sigh was completely authentic as his eyebrows immediately scrunched.

"We better hurry soon, if we're to make it back at a decent time," Philip said before turning around and rolling his eyes.

"Aw man, I hate to hear that. It's been too long since I've been able to talk with my old roommate. I think we all realize that if you don't make time with this guy, you may never get a chance," Benoit exclaimed.

"Of course, I understand, but Philip needs to return soon so he can get some sleep for a conference tomorrow," Sofia explained.

"And my sister has some important work she needs to return to even though she won't admit it," Philip quickly replied.

Without noticing it, Philip triggered an eye roll from his sibling that caught Andres's attention.

"Well, if it must be," Osmond stepped forward with open arms.

"Yes, yes," Benoit responded. "I hope you two find what you're looking for. Especially you, Osmond. This one's never satisfied," he said to Andres while still interlocked with Osmond's arm.

Unbeknownst to the young woman standing beside the even younger man in front of the hugging friends, Philip began to slip down the sidewalk.

It was not until after Sofia embraced Benoit and Andres shook his hand that they all noticed Philip at the end of the block.

The four entered the train and found their seats towards the back of the cabin.

"Perfect, it's not too crowded," Osmond said.

Philip's stare immediately centered to Osmond as he asked, "What is it again that brought you two here? Researching while you travel?"

"Somewhat… yes," Osmond said then looked at Andres. "I'd say it's a similar journey I had thirteen years ago when I was searching for inspiration and knowledge on my AI project. Except this time my project is completed, I have more hair on my chin than my head, and I have help with my research."

"So, you eventually finished your AI model?! That's wonderful to hear. How has that worked out for VIDE?" Sofia asked.

"Great, I suppose. VIDE ended up using my research to develop one of the most interactive security systems to date. A network that can control your household functions, any portable devices, and any automobiles. I recently learned the software has been implemented on a mobile device, but I expect it to be on all systems within the next year."

"Wow, that sounds exciting!" Sofia said before turning to Andres. "So, Andres, what is it you do at VIDE? You seem like an engineer of some sort. You're a young, strapping male… kind of like this old guy back in his hay day."

Andres looked at the friend beside him who chuckled to himself.

"I am an engineer, but an independent contractor on an assignment for VIDE," Andres posited.

"We both are now," Osmond interjected. "Once I returned to Libe Villages, I stopped working full time at VIDE. Now, I take up short-term projects at VIDE or Orion's Eye Observatory."

"Oh, it sounds like you've stayed busy all these years," Sofia said.

Philip, still fixated on Osmond, responded, "That's for sure. If you've finished your AI project, was is it your researching now? Are you developing a new technology?"

"Forgive him, he's only sore because it's been so long since we've seen you," Sofia said.

"No, I understand," Osmond exhaled a deep breath.

While Osmond reached into his pocket, the other three paused and waited in anticipation.

"This," he held his phone on display. "With this, I'll be able to expose my AI system to a much broader audience, outside of my city and even region."

Philip slouched over in their booth seat and gripped his knees with both hands, then shifted his attention to his watch.

"We should reach Llumieres soon," Andres stated.

"Oh, don't mind him. He's simply cranky and tired from our trip. I can't deny Osmond, that certainly sounds like enjoyable research for work," Sofia stated.

"Yeah, I'd say," Philip blurted.

"Yes... well, it's also a nice excuse to see some old friends," Osmond replied.

"Old, huh?" Sofia said as she leaned back and crossed her legs.

"No, I only meant..."

Sofia giggled at the inventor.

"Oh, is that funny?" Osmond smirked. "Hey, I've been wondering for a while now if Benoit ever gave you your necklace back?"

"Benoit? No...I thought you still had it."

"Nah, it had been sitting in our garage when we lived in Cab. I'll make sure to ask him about it when I get the chance."

"Next time you get the chance might be another five years," Sofia quickly replied.

"Yeah, but you'll wait for me, right?" Osmond asked grinning.

"Oh…yes, of course. Llums could probably go without any grand decisions being made for a while."

"See? You're flexible."

"Wish I could say the same for my patience. It's getting a bit thin," she said squinting, looking through her pinched index finger and thumb.

"I apologize, my honor. I didn't realize the great lover of wisdom, my old Lady Lawyer, became judge already. I can practically see the university textbooks that weighed you down."

"Yes, it's like those seven…eight years have just flown by."

Osmond smiled then said under his breath, "It *has* been too long, hasn't it?"

Holding his phone to his mouth, Osmond whispered, "Play that track from this morning."

His eyes turned to Andres as he continued speaking to the phone, "My favorite track, you know the one."

Immediately, a smooth melody comprised of strings rose to the foreground of the booth's atmosphere. With an air of accomplishment, Osmond set his phone down on the window seal as he laid back.

"It looks like your music taste hasn't changed much at all. Can't exactly say the same for your… hair," Sofia said while giving a befuddled look at Osmond's head.

"The light snow, right? Endless nights will do that to you," he replied. "Another factor in my decision to leave my permanent position at VIDE, although I still work many hours with these various projects."

"You sound as if you're ready to retire already. You're not even 40 yet," Sofia said.

"Give it another year, I'll be there. We can't all age with steady beauty, Miss Apiget," Osmond said while leering to the side.

The music stopped as Osmond's phone began to ring.

"Hush and answer your phone," Sofia smiled and leaned back with her arms crossed.

"**UNKNOWN NUMBER**" appeared on Osmond's phone display. A rare sight since he hardly ever offered his phone number.

"I'll be back in a minute. Sorry," he said before walking to an empty section of the cart.

"Hello, who is this?" he asked.

"Osmond?" the voice asked.

"Who am I speaking with?"

"This is Inara. I apologize for the alarm, I know I'm catching you at a volatile time."

"You've spoken with Glen?"

"Yes, he's instructed me to meet you at a location of your choosing. It appears you're not the only one that needs to flee Iri's scope."

Instinctively, Osmond scouted his surroundings before sitting in an empty booth seat.

As Philip stared through the train's glass, he uttered something he thought was to himself, "Ah, I started to like that song too."

Sofia brightened up. "Won't you look at that, Andres? That's possibly the nicest thing my brother has said about Osmond all day. Or possibly decade. What a metamorphosis."

Andres smiled as he quietly replied, "Yes, I have noticed."

"Can you blame me, Sofia? You remember how he left," Philip fired back.

Clearly out of the loop, Andres continued facing forward at the two siblings angrily muttering over events of which he had never been introduced.

"Whatever, he works with him. He can hear if he wants. Andres, what Philip is referencing is Osmond's time in Llumieres. For the two years he lived here, we dated… well, acted as boyfriend and girlfriend. Then one day, the acting stopped. A good thing ended, as they usually do; after all, this is life. It wasn't until he left with our friend, Benoit, to go work in Aryeh that he decided to inform me he was leaving."

"Do you think he might behave as he did when he was last here?" Andres asked Philip.

"Do I think? I'm a behavioral psychologist, Andres. I can't help but believe the *brilliant inventor* has not changed since we last saw him. He's a hedonist, never concerned with the welfare of others. And my sister is a hopeless romantic, which explains her involvement in helping that man achieve his goals."

"You seem to be taking this personally," Andres softly replied.

"As you should, too! I'm not sure of your relationship to him, but I'd be careful if I were you. If he no longer needs you to advance his agenda, he'll be sure to let you know with his absence."

"That's enough, Philip. I think he gets it. Osmond's bad and we should stay away," Sofia waved her hand at her brother.

Andres sat back in his seat and calmly focused on the picture in front of him; Philip with his elbow on the window seal staring into the distance and Sofia lost in a gaze at the floor of the aisle, with her arms crossed. Her eyes were more reflective than usual, akin to two pools of rainwater in the early morning sunlight.

Both siblings shared features that would have instantly alerted any passerby of their relation. Their long hair had a deep brown sheen that shimmered with the dusk that blanketed the train. They each had an iris lightly painted with a smooth umber, a shade darker than their skin. Both were warm models of life's beautifully arranged complexities, hung in a dark tint while on the train.

Andres lingered over the sight in front of him until Osmond broke his stare.

"Hey, what did I miss?" Osmond asked as he sat down next to Andres.

"Oh, nothing. We were just picking Andres's brain on cybernetics and what not. All the stuff you used to go on about years ago," Sofia said.

"Hmm, sounds interesting," Osmond said while turning to Andres, who smiled and nodded.

"It appears we've arrived sooner than expected," Andres stated.

"I'll say," Philip said under his breath.

He then glared at the two in front of him and asked, "How often do you get mistaken for relatives?"

Philip seemed agitated, though this was the most he engaged with Osmond and Andres.

"Often, very often," Osmond replied.

"Yeah, I was kind of thinking the same thing. You two look like long lost brothers," Sofia confessed.

"Nah, I was thinking more along the lines of father and son," Philip stated.

"Phil!" Sofia remarked.

"No, seriously. Andres is almost like a replica of Osmond's youth. Though he's much better looking," he teased.

"Well, thanks…" Osmond gasped. "Glad to see you're finally starting to warm up to me."

Andres stood up. "We arrived in 55 minutes. That's eight minutes quicker than the estimated time."

"Hmm, not bad, eh?" Osmond joked while standing up to join Andres.

Sofia and Philip joined the two in walking to the exit.

"Are you still on that street that Café Stratis is on?" Osmond asked.

"Close, but not exactly. Now I'm at a more suitable residence with a better view of the city," Sofia answered.

"She means a bigger house," Philip stated.

Osmond smirked, "Oh, I see. Always modest."

All four sat in Sofia's living room sprawled out on the two couches. Andres laid nestled in a lounge chair, while Osmond sat opposite from Sofia and Philip. Staring through the window as he had before on the train was Andres.

Few people walked the road in front of Sofia's house tonight. Only a pair of nighthawks populated the air, fluttering about each other in a frenzied tussle. Though each bird spun and twirled around the other, the couple managed to maintain a straight path towards the neighborhood woods.

"Are you a birdwatcher, Andres?" Philip asked as he walked towards Andres chair. "Oh, you're a people-watcher, huh?"

Andres smiled, "Perhaps, I am."

Osmond peeked to his side at Philip's conversation, attuned to each syllable uttered, while barely following the words Sofia spoke.

Philip rested his arm on the back of Andres's chair, "Yes, it's a fascinating hobby. In a profession such as this, you need to be intrigued by people. From their moods, manners, and movements to their ultimate motivations. It's a constant battle that will truly put you to the test."

"How long have you studied and worked in the field of psychology?" Andres asked.

"Thirteen years outside of schooling. It's not until you put the theory into practice that you realize how peculiar humans are. The patterns we tend to play into are an effective way of categorizing us, but when you least expect it, you find that deviant. A small departure from the typical monotony of our mechanical existence. Some strange behavior becomes commonplace and we fuse it to our conglomeration of normality, but the rest... The rest is exemplary of what we truly are; flawed designs scurrying to survive."

"Are you done, Philip?" Osmond asked.

"Seriously, Phil, you sound like a horror track right now. What's your deal today?" Sofia followed.

Flinging both arms in the air, Philip said, "No need to be so critical! I was simply chatting with Andres over the people of Llumieres. You can attest yourself, they're peculiar subjects. And he seems to be interested in human behavior too."

"I am interested in human behavior. It fascinates me to endless bounds," Andres clarified.

"Alright... well, just take it easy at least, Mr. Doom and Gloom. I don't want Andres too bummed out to help with research," Osmond replied.

"No worries, I'm headed to bed anyway." Philip walked upstairs.

Osmond paused for a minute, then asked Sofia, "He lives here now?"

"No, he's only here for his conference. Since he's staying here for the weekend, we visited Benoit. We were lucky to run into the worldly Dr. Diaz and his colleague, Andres."

Restraining his laugh, air pushed through Osmond's nose.

Andres was still engulfed in the chair, facing the window to the street.

"Yup... only luck," Sofia softly stated as she stared at her stairs.

"Something on your mind?" Osmond asked.

"I'm not sure," she let out a deep sigh.

"It's that...you arrived at Cab, the city Benoit works, out of conceivably nowhere. Then you decide it's completely suitable to follow Philip and I along to

Llumieres. What are you doing, and why are you dragging Andres along?"

Osmond glanced at Andres momentarily, then jumped to his feet.

"You can trust her, Osmond. Tell her why you are here," Andres stated.

The gulp from Osmond's side of the room felt like a small bass drum.

"Yes, hun. *Tell me why you are here*," Sofia chuckled.

"Come outside for a second, you need to hear this. And you need to remain quiet," Osmond said while pointing to the top of the stairs.

Sofia stepped outside and immediately shut the door behind her.

"First off, I apologize for throwing this on you so suddenly…"

"Okay, you're starting to scare me. Go ahead and spit it out."

"No, no… Trust me, you can't imagine what I'm about to tell you."

Sofia crossed her arms. "You're not making this sound any better. Tell me, what's wrong?"

"As you can remember, I had been fully immersed in an AI project that I'd hoped would revolutionize the way we interact with systems and the way systems interact with other networks."

"Sure…" she said under her breath.

"Well, I completed that project and performed far more. While living in Cab with Benoit, an even rounder idea revealed itself to me: why create and implement the penultimate interactive software when I can develop hardware to host that genius. Thus, I gave breath to life's greatest achievement!"

The fear from Sofia's eyes grew with her pupils, though Osmond continued anyway.

"At that moment, my life's greatest work became creating life greater than myself."

"Wait… life? You're considering this software as life now?" Sofia asked as her voice rose.

"Yes, life. Of course, it's life. Why would it not be? It's practically the closest thing to a soul we will ever observe in our lives. After all, we're only an amalgam of units arranged to believe we're the Universe's prize. An assembly of materials that store and communicate info. I've simply created a vessel to best hold that info, virtually and physically, data too powerful for our carbon shells."

"Do you mean… you created a robot?"

"An android. Yes… but that doesn't fully explain why I'm here." Osmond paused then inhaled.

Osmond continued, "Because I created an android, it's only natural others are worried."

"Who's worried? Who else knows about this?" Sofia asked.

"Only some close research partners and an acquaintance of Dr. Ehmen Foerde, my financier. The issue is that acquaintance doesn't agree with letting my creation freely exist, thus the reason I stand before you today."

"So, you came here? Where's the android then?"

Osmond's sight drooped down as his hands went into pockets. Silence overtook the two for the next two minutes until a surge ran through Sofia. Her felt terror emanated a heated aura that permeated Osmond.

Still facing the ground, Osmond looked towards Sofia's feet, "Sorry for the surprise."

Sofia turned back to her door and pointed, "That's it, isn't it?"

Her stammered words upset Osmond to his core. He was speechless.

"Andres is your android, isn't it?"

"Right now, there's a research partner of my old colleague headed to Llums. We're going to devise a plan, so we can move forward. Then we'll be out of your hair."

Sofia held her posture facing her door with her back to Osmond.

"This is a lot to process, I need to rest. Turn the lights off downstairs before you go to sleep," Sofia said while opening the door.

She paced through her hall and up the stairs, facing forward the entire time.

Osmond creeped inside with his hands still in his pockets. His movements grabbed the immediate attention of Andres, of which continued to sit in the lounge chair.

"You knew it would be an uncomfortable conversation. There is nothing you can do now," Andres told the lethargic inventor lurching to the couch.

"Andres, would you turn the lights off?"

Andres promptly walked over to the wall. Instantly, both were engulfed in blackness.

"Have a good night, Osmond."

"Ha, yeah. Goodnight, Andres. I have some nightmares to catch up on."

Part Four

TIME

XVI. The Café

KNOCK KNOCK

The house sat still in silence until the knocking repeated with ferocity.

KNOCK KNOCK KNOCK!

"I'm coming in!"

Philip opened the door to Sofia sitting on her bed clutching her legs in a fetal position.

"Sof, what are you doing? You look ragged; did you sleep at all?"

"Yes, I've just been thinking about a lot. Go, go to your conference! I'm fine. I'm going to lunch with Osmond and... Andres. They'll be gone by the time you return."

"Oh, is that what this is about? I told you don't count on him," Philip said.

"Phil, fix your tie and leave. The other stiffs are waiting for you."

"Let me know if you need anything," he said racing down the steps.

As Phil unlocked the door, he glanced at the lifeless body on the couch then at Andres.

"I suppose that one will need some batteries," he said pointing at Osmond.

"I hope you didn't sleep in that chair, that thing is a back-breaker!" Phil exclaimed.

"It's wasn't too bad, I can still move," Osmond grunted.

"Enjoy your conference, Phillip" Andres said.

"Appreciate it! I've got to jet, so try to take care of *that* one," Phil exclaimed before he shut the door behind him.

"Ugh," the corpse said rising from the couch.

"Did that prick finally leave? We best get ready to head out too. C'mon, Andres."

Andres stood up and said, "Where to next?"

"Inara is to meet us at the coffee shop down the street around 8 o'clock. She has something to show us that can hopefully be of benefit for our situation."

The two walked towards the door until Andres stopped in front of Osmond, then walked forward. Osmond glanced at the top of the stairs before following Andres outside.

Inara approached the shop and viewed the sign, "Café Stratis," hanging overhead. Her appearance stole the attention of every pair of eyes caught in an illuminated screen, thus when she immediately went to the center table without a coffee, eyebrows were raised.

Only five minutes after she placed her bag on the floor and sat down, an onlooker from behind timidly approached her.

"I couldn't help but notice when you came in, that is one of the most gorgeous necklaces I've even seen. Where did you get it?"

Inara gently grabbed her golden pendant and gave a genial smile to the young woman beside her.

"This was a gift from my father when I was born," Sofia answered.

"No kidding, it has a vintage look to it, too! I would've guessed it's been passed along a family line."

"Well, it was more of a short family line. My parents shared a matching pair of these necklaces."

The young woman's eyes lit up at the sound of Inara's statement.

"That's so adorable! Wait until you get to share that pair with your own family. I hate bothering you, but it's just you and that necklace are so radiant... like a shimmering light!"

"Thank you, and you've been a pleasure! Don't worry about bothering me, it's no problem."

"You're welcome, lovely. Bye."

As the woman walked away, Inara returned her attention to her satchel, and pulled a dusty, tattered book from the bag.

Before she could split the pages, a tall, stiff figure paused ahead of the shop door and looked up. His presence caught her eye but only due to his sudden movement. That was until a person following the young man approached him from behind. The person behind could have been the young man's father as he was an aged carbon copy.

Both the onlookers peered through the shop's glass with no regard for the returning glares.

While the two looked around the building, Inara grabbed her scarf from her bag and hurriedly wrapped it around her neck.

The two quietly stepped over to Inara's table as she skimmed through her book.

"Hello, Inara?"

Andres approached a display window as Osmond told him, "Wait, this is it!"

Osmond glared through the window at the still coffee-drinkers fixated on their laptops and various black screens. Only one person sitting near the counter had nothing on her table but a paperback block of antiquity she stared at intently.

"That's her, I'm sure of it!" Osmond excitedly told Andres.

"I am assuming you recognize her by her book since you have that same title at your house," Andres said.

"I do. That's the story of a simple technician tearing apart the manipulative controls of his society and creating his own future," Osmond said.

"Yes, she told me she would bring a certain novel. I'd recognize that front cover from anywhere. Plus, I vaguely remember this moment."

"You remember what's happening now?" Andres asked.

"I can't fully explain it, but I think I've seen her in a dream. Sitting in this same coffee shop. At the time, I thought it was someone else but I'm feeling increasingly certain this is that dream."

The two entered the coffee shop and slowly approached the woman reading the book.

Barely able to make out the title since the book was slanted, Osmond read, "of Eternity," the latter half of the book's name.

Osmond asked, "Hello Inara?"

"Osmond," Inara firmly stated, "it's so wonderful to finally meet you. Of course, I've gained an earful from our colleagues, so I've heard a lot about you. And I assume this is Andres, correct?"

"I am excited to meet you as well," Andres replied.

Andres's quick response surprised Osmond, though he continued.

Osmond asked, "Do you mind?" pointing at an empty chair beside Inara. "As you know, we've weaved an exceptional predicament here, so I'm gonna cut straight to the point."

Andres sat down, folded his arms, and crossed his legs.

"You have the disk portion of the 4DM, correct?" Osmond asked.

"The Foerde Manipulator? ...Ha, yes. We'll need to connect it with the part you have to fully utilize it. Solitary, this is simply an energy source."

"I see. I'm not sure if Glen ever told you but he never gave me an explanation of what the device does."

"That's understandable," Inara said. "And no, he didn't *inform* me of its purpose. I helped him engineer this device. In fact, most of its construction is of my conception. Before Iri came into the picture, the only people who knew about the 4DM were Glen, Ehmen, and myself."

He sighed then quietly said, "Let's take a walk. It's a lovely day, nonetheless."

As Osmond, Andres, and Inara stepped outside, Osmond's vision instantly gravitated to the shop's sign above the door.

"Hm, Stratis Café. It's been so long since I've been here, this feels like a reunion. Of all the cities I've traveled to, this is by far the most comfortable place."

"Oh, really?" asked Inara.

"Is that a shock?" he replied.

"I'm surprised an inventor from Libe Villages is warming up to Llumieres, the city of lights. In my experience, most natives of Chun are completely against the lifestyle of Llums. The two regions purport antithetical political, economic, and philosophical positions. From what I've heard, it seemed likely you would be opposed, Osmond."

"Well, you make me sound level-headed when you say that. I admit I'm not a particular fan of this laid-back style of doing things, I mean, there's a coffee shop on *every* corner, but I think I could get used to this area once I'm done focusing on my recent projects."

Inara led the two down the sidewalk for over twenty minutes before she came upon a bench near an empty park.

"This looks like a good spot to talk. I'm sure we'll be ready to take off after things are sorted," Inara said.

Andres stood beside the bench gazing at the trees behind, while Osmond and Inara sat down.

"Things are sorted? At this point, I would assume we have a game plan," Osmond said.

"And what would you *assume* the game plan is?" she replied.

"Well, we first head back to Chun to grab the other part of the 4DM, then we get out of there like there's no tomorrow. Nothing left for us there anyway."

"Incredibly shortsighted," Inara quipped.

"What? Where did that come from?"

"No harm meant. Dr. Kriit somewhat admired that about you."

"Hah, he did? That's past tense…but still sweet."

"Yes, a bit sentimental on his part. He would often comment on how incredibly shortsighted you could be, yet your undoubtable brilliance always outshone your blunders."

"Wow, that's certainly… honest, I guess. I'm not too sure how I should take a comment like that," Osmond said.

"My suggestion is simply take it. Words mean little when actions are present. More importantly, what you plan to do after I explain the 4DM is a decision that will affect more people than you would imagine."

"Well, you make it sound important. Alright, shoot," Osmond replied.

For a slight second, Inara glanced at the optimistic one in front of her as if she wanted to smile at Osmond, but then returned to her stony disposition.

"Dr. Kriit called this device the Foerde Manipulator. Though it's correct in stroking Ehmen's ego, it's better called the 4DM. This device manipulates time and space in a set radius. When activated, the user is expunged from all dimensions of space and time. With this portion of the device, energy is rapidly increased at such an instantaneous rate the user transcends their usual limit of traveling from one point to another unconstrained by gravity and time. Your part of the device allows one to direct their trajectory between any two given points. Clearly necessary if we're to effectively travel unstifled across the fourth dimension."

Andres turned to Inara and said, "Space and time…the great constraints of all life. How momentous it would be to exist outside?"

Osmond depressed into the bench, apathetic to his companion's remark and deflated by his new reality.

"Y'know, this explanation of the 4DM suddenly fills in the gaps I had about Iri's intentions," Osmond admitted.

"I'd hope so. Regardless of what she says, she isn't to be trusted with this device. Dr. Kriit realized the importance of Iri's sudden interest in collaborating with Ehmen, especially at a pivotal time like the present with the completion of Andres."

"*Ugh*, how did I miss a detail that obvious!" Osmond shouted putting his hands on his head.

"I expect your game plan has changed with knowledge of the 4DM. Come," Inara stood up. "I've finished what I came to accomplish and this meeting has expired. Time to take action."

Andres followed closely behind Inara as she made her way to the park's sidewalk, while Osmond pushed himself from the bench, struggling with each step.

"A lot to take in even if the reality was staring me in the face. It's a bit hard to consider heading back to Libe Village now. With a target on all three of us. I don't know how you can stay calm through all of this. You must have nerves of steel," he said.

Inara stopped to respond to the lagging inventor behind her. She looked at Osmond with a slightly understanding expression.

"Preparedness comes from experience," she said. "And distress breeds a terrible amount of experience. Due to the events of my youth in Aryeh, I've built a wall of temperance. Trust me, it's the only way to move when the path ahead is drab and full of cracks."

"Sure…Hey, you grew up in Aryeh?" Osmond asked.

Inara sighed then answered, "Yes, in Cab to be exact. I was orphaned at a young age, so pressure isn't a new element to my table. Now, Osmond."

She stepped forward into Osmond's personal space.

"Aren't you forgetting something?"

The confused inventor stammered, "For-forgetting something?"

"You traveled with some people here, correct? The people that hosted Andres and you for the night."

"Of course, yes, I…"

Osmond looked at Andres who had disengaged from the conversation altogether and was staring at the trees in the park.

After clearing his voice, Osmond said, "I don't think that would be an appropriate idea right now. That person doesn't necessarily want to see me. I kinda tagged along without revealing my intentions of this trip."

"Escape."

"Yeah, our escape. Plus, she wasn't too pleased when I told her about Andres and why we're here," Osmond said before averting his gaze from his inquisitor.

"*Hmph*, oh well then. I suppose we can leave if there's nothing left for you to do here. Come along, Andres. Our time in Llums has ended."

"*SHEESH*, you sound like her. Umm," Osmond mumbled then checked his watch. "If you can allow me half an hour, I can go say 'bye' and meet you at the train station. Does that sound like a better course of action?"

"It does, Osmond. That sounds fine," Inara quickly stated.

Osmond then inhaled a heavy gulp of air and paced down the sidewalk.

"Your explanation of the 4DM answers a previous question I was wondering," Andres stated.

Inara glanced at Andres and said, "Does it? Ha, let's go and wait at the station. I have a feeling this will last a while."

"It would seem you know best."

KNOCK KNOCK

The air inside the house remained still and thick.

"Oh, *c'mon!* Sofia, are you still in there?! *Please* don't say I missed my chance to say goodbye."

The room heated with movement.

KNOCK KNOCK KNOCK

"Sofia!"

KNOCK... KNOCK

"I'm sorry…" he whispered moments before the door snapped open.

Feeling temporarily weightless from the alleviation, Osmond hurried through the cracked entrance.

With her back towards the door, Sofia quietly stepped into her kitchen.

As soon as he entered the house, Osmond reflected on every step behind Sofia, making certain to remain silent until he sat down at the kitchen table.

"You made quite an impression on me, y'know? As soon as I saw you, I felt chills – which is why I considered you might feel the same about me," Osmond said.

Sofia took a sip from the coffee mug on her table while Osmond persisted with his apology.

"I'm sure you realize by now, I love basking in my grief. Watching the flames rise around me is a bit of a masochistic delight, y'know? That probably explains why I enjoy when heavy rains drown all action in an area. The prospect of an oncoming tide to rise me to new heights has always been a temptation of mine. But to see the tide rush over you was never my intention. I'm sorry."

Tears welled in Sofia's eyes, as she hid behind her coffee mug, blinking until she returned to a dry state.

"Thank you…it certainly has been a long time coming. Now what?" she asked staring at the unsettled eyes before her.

"That depends, what do you think should happen next?"

"Oh, don't give me that. Where's Andres? And how did that encounter with the other researcher go? Are you safe now?"

"Well, they should both be at the train station now."

"Waiting on you?"

Osmond shook his head slowly while not breaking his attention on the mug in Sofia's hand.

"You should get back then. I'm certain they're patiently waiting to return to their work."

Osmond smiled, "Y'know, that researcher reminds me of you so much it's scary."

"Oh really… aren't you the lucky guy? More chances than you can count."

Now grinning wider than before, Osmond shouted, "She's far too young for this scientist!"

"Right, because that would be so out of character for you," Sofia said winking.

"Well, I like to connect more with a similar mental age rather than physical age."

"Sure thing, Pops! We're practically the same age."

Both paused and stared at each other from across the kitchen table. The room was still though a current of energy ran from the pairs of glass orbs pointed at each other.

"I'll be back. You don't have to believe me, just know it'll happen."

Sofia slightly grinned, rose to her feet, and walked to the hallway entrance.

Immediately, Osmond followed closely behind.

Before he could react, Sofia grabbed him for a hug. Her head brushed the bottom of Osmond's chin, forcing his silence.

"Before you leave, there's one thing that's irking me. You created a robot!" Sofia shouted.

She lightly hit him in the stomach causing Osmond to giggle like a child.

"*HAH HA…* I know, I know. Honestly, the reason for building him was quite simpler than you'd imagined."

"I highly doubt any reason for creating a *person* is simple!"

"When you put it like that, sure…but if you could do it, would you not?"

"Bye, Osmond. Remember the next time you visit, it better not be dictated by convenience."

"I'll make sure," Osmond said while opening the door.

XVII. Train of Thought

A faint screech from outside the light rail hung overhead the passengers the entire ride, demanding its presence be felt and expected. Among the cart's noises were the constant page flipping of a small child beside their mother and the whistling of an older man in the back corner of the train car.

Osmond felt all the vibrations followed a single pattern symbolic of life's chaotic passions.

Andres and Inara sat in a booth seat together while Osmond slouched in a seat opposite of the two. The flicker of his eyes was a clear indication he would not be attentive for most of the ride.

Andres faced the window in silence as city buildings, monuments, and automobiles blurred by in a flash.

In the booth beside him leaning deep into the seat resting on his arms was Osmond. Since he was low in the seat, sunlight from the window opposite him clashed with his sight, forcing him to squint while observing his companions.

"During the time you left, Libe Villages has been drenched in a terrible onslaught of torrential rains. It took an unsuspected turn from the warm temperatures that had once settled in the area."

"Talk about the weather, huh?" Osmond remarked with a grin.

"I figured you of all people would love to be gifted that news. Even Libe Villages has wept at the loss of your presence."

Lying down in his seat, Osmond restrained his amusement as the beat of his chest dragged to half time.

"Either you're right or the city is cackling itself to tears at my futile actions. Not too sure of either option anymore."

He peeked from between his eyelids as he was suddenly struck by a festering brew of questions and emotions from the young, vibrant woman beside his companion.

"Inara, have I told you yet how much you resemble, my Sofia?"

"*Your* Sofia? No, I do not believe you have."

"The lovely friend it was insisted I go back and thank for the room and board. I met her years ago in the city of lights."

"Oh, so that is the person we waited on for you to thank while we were in Llumieres. I see now. I'm assuming she is a wonderful lady," Inara said with a grin.

"And much more. You two have similar personalities too, so it's kinda neat to watch Andres, arguably the best-looking version of myself, and you, someone as gorgeous as Miss Sofia Apiget, sit beside each other and interact right before my eyes. It's almost like looking at a photograph!"

"It must be quite the experience for you," Inara joked. "I can only imagine the sight of Andres and I takes you down memory lane."

"More than you'd know. It reminds me of a barely noticeable blip in my career when I wasn't wholeheartedly seeking to lay a new brick in the foundation of science. A time when life was undoubtedly vivid with warm edges and no frame."

"You're so fond of the past. Have you thought of appreciating or accepting the future?"

"The future… I'm not certain of its contents, so I don't hope for it. From the looks of it so far, it has its ups and downs," Osmond yawned. "But I certainly wouldn't bet on it."

"Why don't you get some rest before we get to Chun? You seem tired."

Osmond's pinkish eyes became glassier with each yawn.

"Well, I am, Miss Brillar. Unbelievably," he replied.

"The ride to Libe Villages is five hours and thirty-eight minutes from now. That's an adequate amount of time to sleep. I realize you didn't go to sleep until an hour before dawn," Andres addressed.

"Hah, I forget I can't hide anything from you. Yeah, I didn't get much sleep at all last night. Thinking about a lot of things I haven't revisited in a while."

"The future?" Inara asked from the side of her mouth.

"Somewhat, yes. Mostly, what would happen upon meeting Iri."

He quickly sat up to look behind and in front of his seat.

"Now, we're not sure what she's capable of. Especially not when," he nervously checked his surroundings a second time, "that shadowy cult is factored in."

"That's why you must stay vigilant. *We* must stay vigilant." Inara paused and stared at Osmond then softly said, "Osmond…"

The paper whispers of the page-turning child from behind masked Inara's voice and helped lull the inventor to sleep.

Osmond faced the passing structures while his face began to descend. The weight of his head and eyelids increased a thousand-fold, letting his vision be overtaken by the looming black blanket between his eyelashes.

Inara turned from the window opposite of her and looked in Andres's direction.

"He seems placid, so at peace while asleep," Inara said to Andres.

Andres replied, "Yes, he does. The creator of a more advanced consciousness and life greater than his own. It should bring hope for existence that one can see the coming evolution of life. He sees something that many others are unwilling to accept."

Inara sat completely still while her eyes followed Andres's movements. He faced the window in silence as city buildings, monuments, and automobiles blurred by in a flash.

Giggles from behind broke Inara's focus as the young child flipping through a large book played with its pages. As the kid sprung the pages to the right they lowered their face to feel the text's gentle breeze.

The normally poised woman turned around to the child and their mother and asked, "What's the name of that giant book, sweetheart?"

"This is called *Radical Edward*! Have you read it before?!"

"No, I haven't but it seems interesting. Do you mind if I take a closer look?"

"No... here!"

"Woah, this thing's pretty heavy for a person your age. Only a quick kid could grasp a story of a computer hacker. Looks like a difficult read. What's your name, hun?"

"I'm Ash! What's yours?"

"Inara Brillar. This is a research partner of mine, Andres, and that sleeping log over there is Osmond, our research head."

"Cool! You two are very pretty!"

"Ash, hush..." the mother growled and peered at the child.

"No, it's fine. Ash, you're a beautiful soul. Here, I'll have to pick this book up when I get back to town."

Rapidly shifting to the mother for approval, the child happily told Inara. "No, you keep it! I've read it many times. You will like it."

"Oh..." Inara looked at the mother before glancing at the small eyes staring back at her.

"Thank you. You're too sweet!"

Rummaging through her bag, Inara found her excessively tattered book she'd been reading earlier.

"Here ya go. Try this one, it's a page turner."

"Oh, wow! I like this author. He's an old one. Thank you, lady!"

"Not a problem at all. I'm sure you'll appreciate that story. As you can see from the edges, it's my favorite."

"That book is your favorite?" Andres interjected.

"Yes, do you have an issue with that, Andres?" she said turning around.

"No, it's just fascinating. You lived in Mt. Midori before you moved to Libe Villages, correct?"

"I understand, you're still a curious soul. With a little more experience, you'll be up to par. And yes, I *did* live in the Jonglyo region then."

Andres kept his attention on Inara in anticipation that she would continue speaking.

"*Hah*, okay. While in Mt. Midori, I was immersed in a plethora of knowledge, developing simpler meditative techniques while delving much deeper into more complex theoretical physics work. In my downtime, I would also teach at the local youth center."

"That explains your comfortability with that child," Andres said.

Inara chuckled to herself, swaying her saffron curls back and forth.

"Sure, although that child is by far the most brilliant person I've met in a long, long time. Most children are incapable of painting the world with shades of grey. They typically can't understand a story as complex as the blurry ethics of a hacker. But that one... Anyways, another experience of mine that would probably prove beneficial for you is my in-depth research with others. Since you're a robot with artificial intelligence, it made sense for Osmond to equip you with the capabilities of scouring the internet for a near-infinite space of information but working alongside people allows you to experience first-hand the peculiarities of humans. We're all a bit broken, hun. That's what makes us all so similar."

Though his gaze lowered to the floor in a focused contemplation, Andres responded to Inara.

"Yes, in a sense we are all similar, but in a different light as far apart as imaginable. Humans' communication is always parsed due to an imperfect capability to understand and disperse information. When compared to the flawed senses and perceptions humans have, communication between AI seems limitless. Through the internet, direct relations are made by AI. We're capable of action at a distance. This superior method of communication is why AI are typically feared by humans. I expected this fear from humans before I was implemented into this body. I'm finding I'm rarely surprised."

"Hm... I see," Inara smoothly remarked.

In an instant, both were attuned to the booth beside them.

A faint grunt rumbled from the cushions Osmond was squeezed between, a noise reminiscent of a fog horn before dawn.

"Don't worry, it seems to be a dream," Inara assured the perplexed android staring at the sleeping man. "Although, the sporadic jerks are most likely due to a nightmare."

"I know what they are," Andres responded, "but I don't think it's likely I'll experience nightmares for a while. The same goes for dreams as well."

"You may be on to something. Theoretically, if your processing is never at rest, you'll never have a dream. But, if you could achieve a resting state, it may be possible. The typical route for a dream is through its involuntary imagery and emotions while asleep, but there *are* lucid dreams. Hypothetically, if you were in a sleep state while still processing you'd be lucid dreaming."

"*Ughhh*... That was possibly the worst dream I ever had. And it only lasted an hour," Osmond mumbled while stretching.

Inara and Andres glanced at the man now waking from his short slumber.

"Still daylight, huh? I can't wait to return to Chun."

"I assumed you'd be asleep much longer than you were," Andres said.

"Yeah, but you assumed wrong, my friend," Osmond quipped. "First point to note with humans is to never expect a thing. We're a bit chaotic. I can easily say I stopped expecting any outcome a long time ago."

Inara giggled to herself, hiding her face between the window and her shoulder.

"I'm sorry, Miss Brillar. Do you disagree?"

"Oh, don't mind me. I'm just... observing."

"I can see that. Well, now I'm curious. Would you say that humans are random as I make it seem?"

"Are you sure you want my opinion on the matter? I was simply watching the cars pass by and noticed something... humorous."

Andres turned to Inara with the implication of a question.

Inara continued, "I was thinking if that car were sentient? Would it believe it was in complete control of all its actions?"

"I take it that's a hard 'no' to my question?" Osmond smirked.

"Not so much a 'no' as the answer is impossible to determine," Inara replied.

Without warning, the whistling from the old man behind reached a shrieking height then ceased.

"I certainly wouldn't have predicted that," Osmond said while pointing to the old man seated in the back of the cart.

Inara's eyes lowered as her face scrunched to Osmond's words.

"Yeah, I know. Not exactly what you were talking about, but you cannot possibly account for every action a person may choose. The list is endless."

"*Seemingly* endless, yes. But it's a finite list with an extremely low probability of failure. With those odds, it's safe to say we're all beholden to the confines of a determined order."

"I agree with *her!* This woman knows her stuff," the old man shouted.

"Thanks for the reinforcement there, but I don't think so. I'm still not convinced by our wise researcher here. Without fully considering the randomness of particles at a subatomic level, it's reasonable to conclude that the actions of humans are virtually random."

"Sounds like projection to me!" the old man stated then returned to whistling his tune.

Inara briefly sighed before answering, "It may be."

"Improbable, yet not impossible. Theoretically, one could determine every step we were to make. The practicality of someone like Andres or yourself calculating all those possibilities is slim, thus we tend to ignore the notion of quantifying our actions. Nonetheless, we're faced with two truths. Humanity," she then began whispering, "along with Andres, is an amalgam of uniformed chaos that owns the capability of circumventing the expectations of our logic. It is our logic that is the boundary to our actions and thoughts, it completely outweighs us."

"Hmm… You have such a gloomy portrait of humanity, though I can't say I disagree. If you were to classify life, it would sound..." Osmond began to question.

"It would sound like she knows what she's talking about," the old man interrupted.

"Yeah, once again, thanks for that." Osmond rolled his eyes.

"I'm curious where a view like that comes from. I'd expect Andres to view the world in those objective terms rather than you."

"Oh, really? What happened to your lack of expectations?" she asked.

Osmond laid back in his seat and grinned.

"I'm afraid a view like that comes from time," she continued. "A bit cynical perhaps, but it's true. In the grand scheme of nature and consciousness, we're simply flawed machines, and we must learn to live with that truth."

XVIII. Time Stands Still

A slight wind brushed over Osmond's ears as the darkness behind his eyelids blackened further and the shadowy blanket draping his eyes warmed him to a placid state.

"Are you tired, my friend?" a voice asked.

"Hello… Andres?"

"Yes, but I am everyone. I am all, thus I am the one subject."

"Ah… you again?! Last time we spoke, you dragged me on a journey to view events dealing with Sofia. In one of them, she was even shot! What is it now, a vision of my own death?"

Osmond looked around to find the voice until the darkness surrounding him opened to a vast control room with eight chairs.

The two rows of chairs in back were each a row of three seats while the front line had two seats. Each row of seats was separated by a long desk of controls flickering in an assortment of colors.

Trapped in the room was a faint whistle and brush of wind that seemed to forgo Osmond's stay. The whistle was sharp and easily knocked his focus off track.

"What is this place? And who are these people?" Osmond said in a daze.

"You don't recognize them from here? This is the future, my friend. What you saw before were events to come. What you see before you can be called a distant point in your legacy. Only time separates you from here. Now sit back and observe."

Osmond slowly stepped over to the second row of chairs and stared at the two children sleeping, leaning back in the seats.

Both young boys had short black hair and tawny skin that resembled Osmond's tone, aside from their unaged smoothness.

"This is... the future? My future?"

Osmond gently touched one of the young boys' head, observing his peaceful sleep.

"What is the meaning of this?"

"Something tells me you don't know the definition of meaning," the voice whimsically replied.

"What do you mean?"

"Exactly."

Osmond rolled his eyes and said, "Okay... so, I won't get the point since I don't get the point. Got it, totally reasonable."

"Point? You don't need one. No one ever needs a point. They're sufficient, but completely unnecessary. One day what I've showed you will be fulfilled."

The high-energy sound lowered its dynamic and danced a rhythmic melody. Once Osmond noticed the once shrill tone had gradually became bearable, he also became cognizant of the faint brush that earlier swept across his ears had phased out of all recognition. Now only a high pitch song rang in the control room.

All had settled in the room until a hand firmly grasped Osmond's shoulder. The hand – wide and weathered – stretched from an even larger figure in soldier attire, complete with a dark vest and combat boots.

The tall looming soldier had dark golden hair that hung below his ears. Above his breast pocket was a nametag that read, "Gen. Loben." His hardened face gave an adequate explanation of his hard-fought life, and a war story was viewed through each scar that engraved his neck, forehead, and cheek.

"Woah…" Osmond jerked forward. "I'm not used to these…changes of person. Last time you appeared, you were a ship captain or something."

"Is this not the attire of a captain?"

Osmond looked to the room's window and viewed the blackness outside. Only a shimmer of light was seen from the handful of stars in the distance.

"Wait, we're in space?" Osmond asked. He sighed, "On a ship, huh?"

Osmond rolled his eyes and said, "Alright…I give. What is it this time?"

"I told you I am the Infinite Operator. The one true subject. There's no other than me because all are a part of my being."

"Yeah, okay," Osmond said while walking to the plane's back row.

"Does that mean you literally are everyone or is this some kinda metaphor? Over the years, I've become a fan of conciseness rather than this beat around the bush deal."

"Yes, of course. Don't you think I know, my friend?"

In a swift motion, the mellow voiced soldier sat back in the chair beside Osmond. His legs were crossed, and fingers folded.

"I am the only subject because all others are objects including the body I'm now using to communicate with. There can only be one subject. The only interaction by which you see others is through objectification. You, alike all others, are not capable of addressing another as a subject. Mostly because you are literal rearrangements of the same units."

The subject turned his head and looked at Osmond's eyes.

"You have not learned yet to comprehend what I might be," he said in a stern tone.

Osmond felt a chilling shock jolt from his face to his legs. His ankles crumbled as he tried to stand while his thighs froze in midair.

He squatted back in his seat to find the person sitting a mere yard away had disappeared from the chair.

"What…where? You want me to fear you now? Do you not have anything *worthwhile* to give me?!"

"You don't honestly believe that is true. I am the most complex being to date. I have ascended nature to a place where space and time are no longer barriers but are mere options. Fear is to be expected, my friend, as one fears what they do not understand. But I am not seeking your fear. You know that. Now, I am seeking your compliance. Focus."

Making a puzzled face, Osmond looked around the control room for the voice's producer until he jerked back from the face inches from his left shoulder.

The figure now hovering over Osmond pointed to the blue orb approaching the ship.

"What is that place? I've never seen a picture of this planet."

"Yet. You haven't seen it yet... That's Unu, a world of chaos is strangled by structure."

Carefully walking nearer, Osmond approached the front of the ship. He was enamored by the cool, bright color and sheer energy emanating from the cerulean sphere.

"It's mesmerizing! Almost like I'm in a trance."

The constant whistling from earlier that plagued Osmond's psyche finally relinquished its grip, allowing the tired inventor to exhale.

"It seems... perfect. And I feel... amazing."

"It is perfect. It's all perfect. Were you expecting a different feeling?"

"I wasn't expecting anything. The only true way to prepare for the unexpected is to relinquish all expectations. Life births too many inconsistencies."

The subject winked at Osmond then said in a dry tone, "Are there ever truly inconsistencies? I'm sure you realize any irregularities you experience have been written in the script for existence. I assure you the ink is dry, my friend. It has been for a long, long time."

"That's quite a lively picture you paint of existence."

"The picture has already been painted. As it is to come, it has already been finished, and so it shall forever be. We simply mimic its original work."

Osmond's eyes lowered from the radiant blue image to his feet. That moment he wasn't sure what to do next. Though he tried focusing, his thought was in absentia.

"Awake, my friend. Awake to the future," the subject softly said breaking him from his trance.

"Who is that?" a child's voice called out.

Suddenly stunned, Osmond forgot the grand sight approaching and looked to his side while facing forward.

"What's wrong, Ovid? What are you talking about, honey?" the woman sitting in the front row questioned.

"It's fine, I've got this," the man beside her said before getting up to check the child.

"Don't worry about him," the man continued. "That's your father's father, Ovid."

Becoming increasingly perplexed at the situation, Osmond eventually rotated his gaze to the seats behind.

A staring child standing beside his crouching father returned Osmond's glance with precision. The father's face could not be seen behind the desk the child sat at, though his son glared at Osmond with omniscient clarity. His stare pierced through Osmond's body, building a powerful intensity.

Before he could react to the disturbingly prescient, enigmatic youth, Osmond was blinded by a stunning light surrounding his entire body.

A noise akin to a suction cup releasing from the ground sounded from behind Osmond as the blinding light around him honed into a single point in front of him, the wrist of a young man sitting outside on a deck.

The young man tapped his watch. "This is such a beautiful home. But of course, *you* have wonderful tastes."

Osmond looked around to discover he was now standing on a familiar balcony held five stories high.

"This house," Osmond said while feeling the stucco walls.

"This is the home I stayed in during my time in Kadan!"

He hurried in the house to affirm his statements and savor the sight of the old mountainside residence.

"I remember this so vividly. It's like I'm here right now."

"Are you not here right now?" a young man asked.

Osmond ignored the question and continued his walk around the home.

"Oh, come on now. So, what's the reason we're at my old house? Still preparing for the future?"

"You could say that. I'd like to get acquainted with the patriarch of man."

His eyebrows furrowed, and mouth turned agape once Osmond heard the words of the young man.

"That child," he exclaimed, "you're that same kid on the space ship!"

The young man moved closer to Osmond and said, "Yes, my name is Ovid. I wanted to explore the mind of the infamous creator of gods. You may not realize it now, but your reputation will immensely proceed you. Even within other galaxies your legacy reigns prominence. Whether you fully understood your actions is irrelevant. These consequences are what spurred new life. More advanced life."

"What are you saying?" Osmond asked, slightly trembling.

"Eh…it matters not anymore." Ovid glanced at his watch.

"Forgive me in advance if you catch me staring at my watch. Time is easily wasted, and I like knowing what exactly is lost. Do you remember these pictures here?" he asked, pointing at Osmond's walls.

"This one here… The man touching the fingertip of greatness across the background of man's own brain. It spoke to you in ways you did not know at the time, but its resonance contributed in your growth. Growth in creating what would later be known as the one true subject."

"Wait, you're saying I created the Infinite Operator? That hive-mind that torments me whenever I try to rest?"

"Yes, well…torment? I don't think he would consider it as such. And hive-mind is a fair way to describe him. He is pure consciousness, the only wholistic being."

"Whatever he may be, I always manage to meet him in a weird setting like this. Come to think of it, I'm not sure this isn't another of his random meetings. He appears in a different persona each time we meet anyway. I wouldn't know it was him unless he told me."

"Yes, I see. Well, he's literally all, though I haven't heard from him much lately."

Osmond sat down in a chair near the patio.

"You usually talk to him?"

"We typically only interact through talks such as this one. My mother died when my brother and I were little, and my father was forced to travel to handle a matter far away. Eventually, that matter led to his demise and further ascension.

"I apologize if I seem lost, but I am. I'm also sorry to hear about your parents. It must have been tough to only see them in your dreams."

Ovid peered at his wrist until Osmond finished speaking, at which his eyes widened as he drew a blank stare.

"Dreams? I do not have dreams."

Now, Osmond appeared equally as confused as the young man standing before him. Both quickly concluded that they had misunderstood the other and were at a loss of time.

"Did you believe you were dreaming?" Ovid asked as the sounds of a speeding engine overpowered his voice until all that Osmond could hear was the hulking mechanics of a moving cart.

Instantly, Osmond saw a flash of light that covered his entire scope of sight for a handful of seconds. The light quickly rose to a single point beaming from the sky as Osmond scrunched his arms in a feeble attempt to block the rays.

Once his eyes adjusted to the area's light, Osmond realized he was laying on a light rail seat beside Andres and Inara.

He wondered about the dream he had and whether it was really a dream.

He checked his watch to see only an hour had passed since he last looked at the sight of his two friends sitting in the next seat. While on the ship and in the Kadan house, only a single hour had passed.

Osmond shouted, "*Ughhh…* That was possibly the worst dream I ever had. And it only lasted an hour."

XIX. Homebound

Osmond stepped onto the sidewalk and into the nearby trimmed grass. Heat visibly rose from the cement path and caressed all that walked by.

"Oh wow, I almost forgot how Chun weather feels. I've been pampered by the northern breeze of Llums," he said, stretching.

"Alright, we should probably head to your house as quickly as possible. I'm sure Iri's associates have *inspected* the area by now," Inara stated.

"You don't think she's gone through my house, do you?"

"The Prime Minister is no pushover. I'm sure as soon as she learned you were ditching her surprise meeting she went on the offensive. That goes for Ehmen as well. I haven't heard from him since he warned me, but I can be certain the Prime Minister had a tense talk with Ehmen."

"Ugh, that's right. Ehmen did stick his neck out for us. It would be quite the sunken cost if the 4DM or Andres were to be taken after so much has been sacrificed by so many people. Let's move."

"I'll call Ehmen to let him know of our next steps," Inara said while dialing on her phone.

Andres and Osmond walked beside the edge of the sidewalk with Inara closely behind.

The murmur of Inara's phone call was faintly heard by the two in front.

The sidewalk was littered with grass that burst through the cement cracks and crevices left unattended.

"Y'know, it's funny. Only a week ago, I was considering my long-improvised plan of escorting this newly created life across the different regions. Assumedly, we would travel to the vast sand-covered region of Aryeh, tour the northern reaches of Llums and all its glory, then venture to the far eastern region of Jonglyo to see the diverse landscapes and infrastructure. Observing and interacting with a plethora of things would certainly excel your learning to unreachable heights in a matter of weeks. But it'd seem most of that traveling has been taken care of due to this conflict with Iri."

"Are you suggesting my experiences have already assisted my intelligence beyond expectations?"

Osmond remarked, "Of course, I'd honestly say you surpassed humanity when you were simply AI confined to my home network. I often choose not to reflect on my past actions. Regret and reverence hold no weight on the present if one is to be truly free."

"That sounds dangerous. That cannot be a good course of plan for learning."

"Well, I never said that method was for everyone, y'know?"

The three came to a rest once they reached an empty intersection. A sign for **Libe Villages** was placed on the side that read it was five miles further west while a sign for **Dwa** led north thirteen miles straight. Though a few cracks remained on the sidewalk's path, the street had mended itself near the lampposts. In the center of the intersection was a smoothly paved path, fresh and free of fractures.

"Not much further from here, though I'm not telling you anything new," Osmond said.

Osmond continued as before, "The massive potential AI holds for innovation, the substantial increase in efficiency. It's of course a looming danger for humanity. In no way can a human compare to the grand complexities AI warrant. Whether we will admit it or not, even our creativity will be overstepped by technology's next advancement. What abstract concept could humans possibly conceive that can't be replicated in simple logarithmic terms? Persistence of human superiority is futile as the inevitable takeover awaits."

"You seem to take the replacement of human production a light event. Is this a sincere position you have on humanity's existence alongside AI?"

"Sincere? Hah, what's sincere is the notion that humanity will exist beside AI. The eventual takeover of Juk by cybernetic forces will eventually become vocal of the wasted resources humans constantly devour. Land, water, other life…even the air is consumed en masse by us."

"What do you suppose will happen with the continuance of human beings?"

"You ask many questions for which you have an answer. I expect nothing less from you," Osmond said. "I understand. I'm also not quite sure which is a greater pleasure. Watching a person gestate on an answer or actually learning the answer."

"We're about to pass my house. It's on the next block and the first on the right," Inara said.

"You live in the same neighborhood as me? I had no idea! And this whole time we never met in person. Such a shame," Osmond said.

Inara said, "I guess that goes to show the patterns in everything. Life's full of structured gifts simply waiting to be deciphered."

"With an outlook like that it must be easy to view the beauty in ordinary things, no?" Osmond questioned.

"I suppose," she said under her breath.

"Oh, come now. You sound so drab about it," he replied.

"And it sounds as if you've never experienced a person you couldn't read like a textbook."

Osmond said, "Then you'd be correct. I'm pretty good at reading the depth of a person."

"If you say so."

"Oh, you don't believe me? Try me then Miss Brillar."

"How, you want me to ask you a question? You actually want me to put you to the test?"

At that instant, Osmond took a long stride over a puddle covering a meter of the sidewalk. Andres's footsteps splashed in unison as Osmond passed by the water. Inara followed behind Osmond's movement leaping over the puddle.

"Go ahead" Osmond boldly stated. "I bet I could tell you something about yourself before you guess anything about me. Go ahead, ask away and I'll ask you something."

From the corner of her eyes, Inara peeked at the two in front of her as they continued their pace through the neighborhood.

"A bit confident, I see. What would you say if I asked you why I'm helping you two? I could easily be sitting somewhere unknown to everyone we know and let you determine your own fate."

Andres let out a short snicker at the question while Osmond rolled his eyes and looked away.

"Well…" Osmond lingered on the question.

The sidewalk Osmond, Inara, and Andres had been pacing on finally came to an end as the trees along the path grew with a healthy depth and vacuous shade.

"Alright, I'll run in and you two can stay here," Osmond said while creeping through his front yard.

"Nonsense, we're going in with you. There's no telling what's inside there. It's naïve to believe that the Prime Minister hasn't taken preventative steps to avoid triggering any security measures you have. Come on, Andres!"

Careful not to make any noise while turning his key and door knob, Osmond sunk into his door, slowly brushing the floor.

Though he implemented the utmost delicateness with cracking the entryway, the door slammed against the wall as Osmond's arms fell to his sides.

Andres stepped into the house ahead of the stunned figure at the door, stepping on broken glass and clumps of pillowcase feathers.

"They broke everything," Osmond said, dragging through the salon.

"I'll check the other rooms!" Andres stated while walking down the hall.

Panicking about his living room, checking every broken statue and cracked vase, Osmond's eyes rushed around the room in search of a reason.

Storming through the kitchen cabinets and shelves, Osmond suddenly froze from a streak of terror.

He paced through the front part of the house to the guest room in a constant stride.

Inara observed in wonder until the inventor disappeared in the room.

She glanced at her watch then sat down on the couch.

Talking loud enough to echo throughout the entire house, Inara yelled, "When you've felt the effects of both sides of the coin, you're no longer unsettled by the toss of the flip, Osmond."

No response emerged from the room Osmond was in, though Inara continued as if she knew she was heard.

"You provide far more than meets the eye. I'm sure most wouldn't peg you to own as many works of art as you have here. You tend to come off as the silent scientist that never concerns himself with fanciful creations. You have so many works with the intention of entertaining and evoking emotion rather than nudging humanity's advancement with nature."

Still indifferent to the person speaking to him from the living room, Osmond hurried to his basement.

Osmond ran downstairs to find the thick steel door with various locks had been cracked, an opening slightly large enough for a person to enter sideways.

In the salon, Inara crossed her legs, rested her hands on her lap, and stared at the painting above her.

Since her head leaned back over the top of the chair, her voice expanded across the room.

"But of course, I'm not most people. I could read you as soon as we met. I could tell you are *still* deeply invested in Sofia. Your emotions for her might be hidden from all others, including Sofia, but those feelings ring loud and clear to me."

Careful of each step he made on his toes, Osmond peeked around the door into the laboratory space.

Everything appeared still and intact to him, contrary to every thought that rushed through his mind.

The air felt cool and placid in all but one place in the laboratory. To the right and behind the entrance emanated the vibrations and energy of a neurotic stranger.

Osmond could no longer tip-toe around the issue and flung forward to confront the movement.

"Hello Osmond, have you found anything out of place?"

"Andres, what are you doing in here? No, better yet, how did you *get* in here?!"

"You have a biological scanner locking the door, and you gave me DNA, presumably to coexist within humanity. The only obstacle between me entering this laboratory was rearranging my DNA like yours."

Andres held his hand up in front of Osmond then turned around to attend to the table behind him.

"Oh, yes… I guess that is… possible. Never an intention of mine, but I guess that's how that goes," he muttered under his breath.

"This part of the 4DM seems to be in working condition. It's energy level seems unchanged and still able to be attached to its connecting piece."

"Alright, let's take off then."

Osmond paused and scratched his head before turning to Andres's face.

"Y'know, I hate that the idea has just occurred to me, but I think I have the answer to our problems. Why flee the area when we have the greatest vehicle across space and time, as well as the device's initial operator?"

Andres moved closer to Osmond and whispered, "What should we do now? Do you think Inara will be open to trying your idea?"

The absent expression from Osmond was the answer Andres had not expected.

Andres placed the 4DM back in its lockbox and began to head out of the lab until he paused in front the doorway.

"If this was all we needed, what were you searching for earlier? You seemed frantic when you hurried to the guest room," Andres said looking back at Osmond.

"Just securing my future, y'know?"

POP... POP!

Andres immediately glanced behind him with uncertainty.

"That came from upstairs. Inara!" Osmond shouted running passed Andres. "C'mon, nothing good could have come from that sound!"

Andres dragged behind his companion as they merged with the shadows upstairs.

XX. And Space

Osmond inched into his hallway connecting to the salon, and with extreme caution checked every centimeter of the carpet.

The air was thick and smelled of burning metal, while the rumble of a heavy voice could be heard mumbling in a language Osmond had rarely heard.

Andres placed his hand on the hallway wall before the living room and stood still.

"I can feel there are two people in the living room," Andres said standing quietly.

As Osmond peeked his head around the corner of the hallway, a colossal man burst through the front door and bolted into the street. The image of the giant figure dressed in all black imprinted on Osmond's mind, amplifying the chills already riddling his spine.

Andres stepped in front of Osmond and entered the living room.

Still hesitant, his nerves rapidly fired, though Osmond crept into the room behind Andres.

"Where is she?" he asked through a frightened, crackling voice.

Andres pointed to the couch, at which Osmond kneeled behind the couch with his hands gripping the top of his head.

"What have they done?"

He held the back of her neck holding her limp torso in his arms.

Inara's hair draped her face and her arms fell by her side, lifeless, cold, and distant.

"Wha-what do you think we should do with her? We can't leave her here," Osmond said through a cracked voice.

"Don't worry, we'll be alright," Andres answered.

Andres headed to the splintering slab that was once a front door.

"This is my fault?" Osmond whispered to himself before twitching and falling to the floor.

All in one motion, the lifeless body in Osmond's arms jerked from his core and scrambled to its feet before him.

Inara stood above Osmond and brushed her hair from her face.

"Did that ingrate leave?" she asked.

Osmond blankly stared at the dead body that rose in front of his face. He sat neatly on the floor behind his couch, all-the-while glaring at the vivacious shell.

"Yes, I was meant to tell you much earlier, but the time needed to be exactly right or else we might have suffered unforeseen consequences."

While speaking, she pulled a tiny flattened lead cylinder from her shoulder and peeked at the hole in her stomach displaying a tiny blue spark atop a dark metal sheet.

"He truly did get a great shot at my vitals. I suppose we can patch that up later, huh?" she asked, giggling.

"So, you're a robot? This whole time…while you worked at VIDE and the Observatory. No one knew?"

"No, I haven't told anyone. And I'm sure it's a bit unnerving to find out someone you were learning to trust has been withholding a huge secret this whole time. Please don't be too upset."

The curious android lingered at the doorway waiting for the next prompt from the two inside.

"Iri most likely realizes by now. We should leave soon since it's now known we've returned to Chun," Andres said.

"Osmond… Andres's right. We need to get out of here."

A small, dainty hand extended in front of Osmond's face, though his focus was grounded. With the gathered news from the past five minutes, Osmond felt entitled to an additional length in time.

"Let's move," Inara repeated to the wide-eyed inventor.

"Unnerving? You can't be serious" Osmond laughed.

Inara lifted him to his feet while clinging tightly to his arm and coached him to the door.

"I won't let you fall again," she whispered still clutching his limp body.

While walking onto the front yard, Osmond broke away from the arm lock with Inara and paused at a tree in his yard. His breathing was impeded and noticeably weak.

"Alright, stop! We're not moving until I get some answers!" he shouted.

"Osmond, now is not the time or place to discuss this," Inara fired back at the neurotic man leaning on a tree.

"Well you'll have to *make* it the right time *and* place! Why are you not dead on my living room floor and most importantly, who are you?!"

"Calm down, Osmond," Inara said while walking along the sidewalk.

"You're asking questions to which you already know the answers. Of course, I didn't detail my cybernetic components or explain my agenda, but I needed to hide my purpose to reach my objective."

"Oh no… Ehmen was right about my decision. I messed up," Osmond said, gripping his head in a wild fit.

"No, you're wrong. It was never your decision," she rebutted.

As Inara walked down the sidewalk behind Andres, Osmond followed the artificial lifeforms leading his way.

"You can't possibly believe this is all due to your creation of Andres. The universe is far greater than a single life on a particularly fruitful rock."

"Is that it? All that has happened with Iri and me was subject to your will. Are you not running the show here, fulfilling your *objective?"* Osmond asked.

"My objective was to help in the creation of the 4DM and protect you!"

Osmond's knees locked, and his face went expressionless.

"Protect me from what…?" he sullenly asked.

Inara turned around to the stunned individual with an agape mouth and reached towards her stomach. She pulled out a metal crumb, equally corroded on all sides.

"I needed to protect you from the horror that would have ensued if penetrated by this sliver of malice."

She then draped the wound with her jacket and dropped the crumbled piece of lead on the ground to return to Andres's shadow.

"Wait," Osmond scurried behind Inara who was leading the way while numb to his helpless demeanor.

"If you were protecting me, you knew Iri was planning to confront me back there. Why go through all of that if you were aware of the future?"

"Who's to say I know the final outcome of Iri's actions? I knew the exact location and time of her arrival but what was to come afterwards remained elusive. I'm simply trying to protect you because you're too stubborn to accomplish it yourself."

A brief snicker emerged before Inara as the three continued down the sidewalk, focused on their destination.

"I'm glad you're taking this new advancement so well. Since you two seem to be on the same wavelength, would you mind telling me where we're going?"

"We're heading to the light rail. From there, we can travel to an Eastern region far from Iri's watchful eye," Inara said.

"I suppose if you think she'll stop pursuing us we'll be fine; however, I doubt that will be the case. It'd be best if we informed Glen of our whereabouts and well-being. As the minutes pass, I'm believing more and more our meeting with Iri is inescapable."

"Assuming you're right, we should prolong that inevitable meeting," Inara replied.

"Glad we're on the same page. Now, if you'd humor me with an answer, tell me how you know of my supposed fate. You've seen the future, right? Your foresight ranges far wider than my imagination lends," Osmond sternly questioned.

"Perfect, you see ahead? Let's hurry, we can use this bus to reach the light rail," Inara said.

"Hello?" Osmond asked again.

Inara and Andres raced onto the bus in step with a speedier tempo and sat in the back seats. Only the driver accompanied the three journeyers.

"Back where we started, on the run," Andres said from the side of his mouth.

As Osmond tensely began to open his mouth in clear frustration, he was stopped shortly by Inara.

"Alright, settle down," she stated.

Since Andres sat next to the window and Inara on the edge of the seat, she rotated to Osmond in the seat beside her, while staring at her shoes.

"I apologize if I come off as rude but you're getting unnecessarily excited," she said.

"What? Seriously?!"

"Have you not realized by now, I'm usually serious. The 4DM we have now isn't the first one I've interacted with. Yes, the answer you're looking for is that I traveled here with the 4DM in hopes of bettering this instrument and slowing Iri from stopping the human that gave birth to this all. I couldn't let her destroy humanity's greatness."

"Humanity's greatness, huh? I'll admit, that's quite the cause. I'm flattered, but still," Osmond said looking away, blushing. "Wait…if that's the case, the 4DM works. That means we can travel anywhere, any when."

"Possibly," she replied, exhaustingly.

"There's no guarantee. When I first used the 4DM, I planned on traveling to the exact spot that goon attacked you. I instead arrived in Aryeh thirteen years ago. After the trip went awry I decided it'd be best I kept the device that erred and contribute to Glen and Ehmen's work in completing their new budding development."

"So, you're the reason for this project's success. Hm, that's strange. Because of its failure you could complete it. Well, possibly. If you worked on it, traveling with it shouldn't be of any concern. After all, your programming will not let you fail, right?" Osmond asked.

"That's how a robot created by you would act. They would be centered on their objective," Andres said holding the lockbox in front of him.

"Typically," Inara quickly responded.

"Oh, no, not this again," Osmond sighed.

"I've been around artificial intelligence for the past decade, yet this is still surreal. I can only imagine how poor Sofia felt. She never signed up for any of this."

"I meant that typically a robot created by the great Dr. Osmond Diaz would be wholeheartedly focused on their objective but not in this case."

A noticeable question mark formed across Osmond's face.

"This case?" he questioned.

The bus rocked the inventor around in his seat almost flinging him from his row. Inara and Andres stared as Osmond was forcibly shook.

Andres appeared uninterested, while Inara gave a pitiful glare.

"Yes, in this case you might have become too emotionally invested with your creation," Inara whispered across the aisle.

"As I said before, I traveled from a time and place in which you were killed by Iri. In that time, you created a robot like the one here, but you modeled its design and personality from a different person than yourself."

Osmond tunneled himself into his seat by pushing the floor, backing up with his feet. His arms folded as he pouted and stared at the floor.

"I created you…didn't I?" he asked.

His question echoed, vibrating from his head to his fingers and toes. The answer reverberated throughout his body in that moment.

"Actually," she responded with a faint smile. "That's a complex question. I wouldn't put it that way."

"In what way do you mean? How else can it be put? It's kinda black and white. Either I engineered a robot I had no idea about this whole time or…well, I don't know."

"If you could calm down, I can explain it in the best way possible."

"Well, I'm all ears."

"I apologize for not telling you much sooner. Before the idea of Andres, there was me. I'm not sure if you're beginning to catch on, but the inspiration for my design is attributed to your… devotion for Sofia."

Osmond held eye contact with Inara while squinting as if the sun's rays shaded his foresight.

"You couldn't possibly expect Sofia to stand by as her love was fatally struck. Likewise, I cannot and will not allow anyone to hurt the father of my being. I guess that was the initial flaw in your creation."

"No, I wouldn't say that about you," Osmond said, staring at the ground. "Because of your attachment my life was saved. I assume that has to be of *some* worth."

"Yes, that is one way of understanding it. I've been harboring this secret for quite some time now. It isn't something I originally intended, but I adapted to the situation," she said. "But I should have you know, what's to happen next is completely beyond my scope. I can only hope for the best."

Osmond grasped his forehead while the two in the seat beside him stared.

Andres asked him, "Are you alright?"

He turned to the window behind him and murmured, "Ugh…sure. I guess I have no choice."

Part Five

IDEAL

XXI. The Answer

A weighted thud reverberated through the greyish lobby and shook the thin office doors when a statuesque figure dressed in all black paced through the hallway. His dark suit contrasted with the pale walls, framing a giant ink blot that scurried across the giant canvas wall.

"Hello, Madam?" the visitor asked knocking on the hallway's last door.

His speech left deep cracks in the drab door that was absent of color.

"Mr. Straz, is that you? I've been waiting for quite some time," a smooth, delicate voice said from behind the door.

"Come in."

"Madam Prime Minister, it's a pleasure to return. I'll be concise, I have some unexpected news," the hulking figure said while bowing with his hands behind his back.

"Oh, come now. I'm sure it's not as surprising as you make it seem."

"I reached the Diaz residence and encountered another instead of finding the android, ma'am."

One of the Prime Minister's dark eyebrows rose above the brim of her glasses, effectively responding to the confessing brute.

"It was the young lady you met in the hallway at VIDE corporation. The timid one with the brownish golden hair," he said in a perplexed tone. "Or it could have been a bright brown color, I'm not sure."

"Oh… how observant of you. Of all people, I wouldn't expect you to catch the minute details," Iri said rolling her eyes.

"Yes, I remember that girl. She was a bright, young beauty. I…didn't realize she was working with Dr. Diaz and the android. What did she have to say about the two?"

Iri's question hovered over the shadowy man crouching in the chair before her.

"Hello…Vladimir? Was my question not clear? What did that young woman say?"

He subsequently flashed his line of sight to the bottom of Iri's desk then raised his head, ready for the inevitable response.

"Upon arriving, Madam, the young woman in question immediately told me Andres had left and his whereabouts were unknown. It was an intensely strange sight. Almost as if she was waiting for me to arrive."

Gravity dragged Vladimir's head back to the comfortable point in front of Iri's desk.

"Why do you seem so upset? We can still find him. Right, Vlad? We *can* still find the android, right?"

Iri sighed, then asked, "What's wrong?"

After searching the room for an even safer spot to take refuge in, Vlad finally connected with the amber eyes staring at him.

"She's *dead,* Madam," he confessed with a crackle.

"Once she told me Andres had left I was suspicious. She then said something about it not working this time.

That *you*, Madam, would not hurt Osmond this time. It was a strange, wild rant."

"I'm not hearing the part explaining her death. Why is that?"

"Yes. At that point... she approached me."

"Approached you? Vladimir Straz, are you telling me out of pure *fear* you shot a defenseless young woman? You're five times her size. What could she have done?"

"No, Madam. I am saying I shot a robot that proceeded to approach me."

Already standing at attention before Vlad finished his sentence, Iri held herself with both arms attached to her desktop. Her focus was enhanced to the fullest, emphasized by her now still crimson braid. Until then, the fiery rope of hair swung modestly, but consistently.

"What do you mean? Please, explain."

"That's what surprised me about the girl... She seemed exceptionally normal until I noticed something strange about her mannerisms."

"Yes? And what of her mannerisms?"

"She had none. Her demeanor was incredibly strange for a person whose home was just intruded. It was almost eerie. Because of her unyielding stoicism, I performed an x-ray scan."

He held a hand over his right eye and slowly massaged his cheek bone.

"All mechanical components. She was made *entirely* of metals, more than anyone or anything I've ever encountered," he said, lowering his hand to reveal a glowing red iris emanating distress from every angle.

Iri stepped to the side of her desk and looked at the scarlet clock above the door.

"At what time did you leave the Diaz residence?"

"It has been exactly one hour and thirty-four minutes since I left the sidewalk in front of the house."

"That means they've had that much time to scramble and devise a plan. Not a position we want to be in. Stay here and listen in on any communication received. I'm sure Dr. Diaz is bound to reach out to someone. At that point, we can track him and end this danger."

"Alright, Madam. I won't fail you again," he said, rising to attention.

"Oh, I know there's no need to worry. You always produce results. What does worry me is the amoral developer of a life he's not willing to be responsible for. With his apathetic attitude towards society, he poses a greater danger than the robot he's created. A powerful body like that unguided by a soul is a threat to all life."

"I couldn't agree more, Madam."

"It's time we pull out the big guns," she said, staring out the window.

Her hands held her hips forming a formidable stance, only rivaled by the swing of her rouge braid.

Pointing out the window, she shouted, "There! We'll set up in the following neighborhood. He'll have no choice but to succumb."

"Honestly, it baffles me also, Madam. Why would he devise such a creation? It will inevitably overtake him without him ever expecting it."

"That's the stubbornness of men for you." she giggled while starting down the hallway.

"For a human to create such an image that would necessarily balloon all others, is selfish. The man's a fool attempting to house his ego in a lively statue of his own recognition. No one knows what's to come of his egoism."

"No need to worry, Madam. I won't fail you again."

"Oh, you never have, my dear," Iri said pacing down the blank hallway.

Her crimson hair bounced between her shoulders in a tight braid like a pendulum of dark fire. A harsh, precise knock rang with each step she took along the hallway. She was a spark that illuminated every inch of the dry, white plaster on each side of her.

One person stood at the front door as Iri glided by to the exit.

Never did her tempo slow while moving from the hall, through the door, and onto the street.

Outside, she paused on the sidewalk near a stop sign and promptly unveiled a cigarette.

Within two seconds, three cloaked figures in all white surrounded her. One reaching towards her hand stated, "Let me light that for you, Madam!"

The other two hunched just out of Iri's eyesight, carefully watching her face, waiting for her eyebrow to budge or her cheeks to shift.

They were disappointed as Iri looked above her to the sign standing overhead.

"Thank you, my loves," she said, still avoiding eye contact with the hooded men around her.

A bright film seeped from her mouth and formed a cloud around her head.

"Ugh," Iri sighed, "how could he? Tell me, where are the others?"

"The two in Libe Villages have moved to Orion's Eye with our larger group," one of the cloaked figures muttered.

The person in front of Iri still holding a lighter turned to his white-draped peers with a distinct pause then asked, "That makes about 55 then, right?"

"I'm not sure."

"No, I believe so."

"Should we even join them then?"

"There's already so many, we'd add little importance."

"Yes, you're probably right."

"I agree. There might even be too many there now."

"Are there? That seems like a round enough number to occupy the area."

"Well then, problem solved."

Iri's head leaned back on her shoulders as she rolled her eyes and puffed out smoke above her head.

"Are you done?" she asked before putting out her cigarette on the sign behind her.

"Time is the only matter we need to solve now," she said tugging at her watch's wristband. "Report!" she blurted while glancing down the street.

"Yes, Madam!"

Without a moment to think, the one nearest to Iri replaced his lighter with an illuminated mobile phone.

"Calling them now, Madam," he said, holding the phone in front of the fire-tipped femme.

"Hello, Sven? Are you there?" the phone asked.

"This is Iri, hello."

"Oh my… Good evening, Prime Minister. How are you doing? Is there any way I can assist you?"

"There absolutely *is*. I'm looking for our dear friend…um, Victor and his creation."

"Victor… Vic- oh, yes! Right… Victor."

Iri let out a deep gasp and asked, "Do you still have eyes on them?"

"Yes, Madam. We've been following them since their departure from Libe Villages. So far, they've visited the Orion's Eye Observatory and VIDE corporation, and I believe they may be on the move again."

"Hmm… well, they're certainly fond of traveling. Do you know of any reason why they might be moving now?"

"My partner has been listening closely during both visits. On what we've gathered, the three are headed to one of Victor's friends."

"Three, huh? I'm assuming the third you speak of is a young woman a bit shorter than me? With golden hair?"

"Correct, Madam. And she appears to operate very strangely. Every location my partner and I have been at, it seems she has managed to spot us."

Iri's hand covered her mouth as she snickered at the previous comment.

"I bet she does *operate* pretty strangely."

"Madam?"

"Never mind the girl, where do you suppose they are headed, my dear?"

"Well… from the looks of it, they seem to be going straight towards Aryeh."

"Oh really… in search of a friend in this ancient region? Hm, I'd expect his friends to be a little more creative than," she paused to glance behind her before saying, "this place."

"Since Victor and company are traveling in your direction, should we all return to your office?"

"Yes, of course. I'd love that, my dear. We'd all love that," she said, winking at the three beside her.

The phone screen blackened and all sound on the sidewalk ceased for a moment.

"Evan, Tin...um, you three follow me. I need another briefing on Victor, so I can understand why his movements seem so erratic. And maybe learn who's controlling who."

"What about Aete, Madam?"

Squinting at the person cloaked in white, Iri hesitantly answered, "Yes, sure. Aete included."

While walking down the street, sunlight skipped over the tops of their heads and reflected a blur of pink alongside the shop windows.

"Our records show that Victor's first interaction with Ehmen-" he said, suddenly cut short.

"Code names, my dear. Code names."

"My apologies. Victor's first interaction with Twissell endured through their time in university until about thirteen years ago."

As they walked towards the evening sun, the light surrounding them intensified and their figures increasingly grew darker. Color drained from their silhouettes into the dusk's grand performance.

XXII. Cybernetics and Coffee

A high-frequency chime rang as Osmond held the rustic diner door open for his orderly companions.

"This place is considered a crossroads between Aryeh and Chun. I used to frequent this diner when I first moved to Cab."

Looking around the quaint restaurant's floor, Inara said, "I'd be remised to not mention it's… exceedingly aged appearance. It's a salient example of Aryeh."

"Hah, agreed," Osmond said.

"This is quite the timepiece," he said, directing the two to a booth near the corner of the restaurant.

"But you should be wary of conflating this establishment with the average image of Cab. For a city in Aryeh, Cab is a diamond hidden in a barrel of coal."

"Visitors to Cab, huh? You sound like the tour guide for these young faces," an older man said from the booth behind them.

"Yes, they're new to the entire region. The entirety of their time spent here has been in a seat speeding by in a couple hours."

"Oh, really?! Well, you two are in for a treat. Living in Aryeh lends a much slower pace than any other region. The infrastructure is typically cracked and dried since yesterday's customs have for a long time muscled out the advances of today. That and the incessant sunlight."

The older gentleman began framing his sentences with his hands, "Notice how vehicles are powered by petroleum and streets are outlined by sands. Keeping up with the steel-enforced industries of today is of no concern to the modern Aryeh collective."

"But Cab, the grand megacity of the past is incomparable to any other place in all of Juk!" Osmond exclaimed.

"Your friend is right, no exaggeration either! Cab offers a unique blend of cultures, blurring the grains of time."

During the conversation surrounding him, Andres remained silent and looked forward. Only the diner's window and the street outside were in his line of sight.

"Let's see," Inara said, propping up a menu on the table with full focus of its contents.

"Oh, sorry, don't let me hold you fine people up. Youth is a gift, you'll have to explore to unravel its present. Don't waste any time, especially not on my account."

"Well, thank you, sir! We've been traveling for a while, and I'm sure these two are starving," Osmond said with a grin.

"One thing I'm especially hungering to hear are the details to that dream you mentioned earlier." Andres said.

Andres shifted his attention in that moment, locking his eager eyes with the inventor across the table.

"Yes, I'm also interested in hearing that story." Inara said. "You've never mentioned your dream to me."

"Ah," Osmond sighed. "That's probably for the better. I guess it explains why I'm sitting across from the two of you right now."

"So, you had a dream that influenced your creation of…" Inara looked at Andres then said, "us?"

Osmond leaned back in the booth and folded his arms. The slight grin he held was a signature Andres recognized early on, a characteristic he perfected that Andres now expected to find every so often.

"Hey, how are you doing?" Osmond asked the waitress, while still holding a simper.

"We'll have one plate of scrambled eggs and potatoes, and a small slice of cheesecake. Cheesecake, right?"

"Yes, that's fine," Inara answered.

"Alright, that's fine. Thank you! I swear…I don't recognize any of the employees here anymore, though it has been some time since I've visited."

Now nestled back in his seat, Osmond noticed he had the patience of the two pairs of eyes staring back at him.

"Let me just preface, it's not a particularly great story, but I'm now learning its true significance. The Infinite Operator… he's long appeared to me. I was just unaware."

"The Infinite Operator. That is the same name you described before, which came to you during your sleep. What were the details of the dream?"

"Ah, let's see… Well, from what I remember, it first started similarly to the last one. I heard a strangely soothing voice reach out to me from above, like a telepathic intercom. Of course, at this point, I had assumed my own insanity."

"Please forgive my interruption," a strained voice urged from behind. "But your mystery voice from above reminds me of someone."

"You've had a similar dream?" Inara asked the older man.

"No, I've never had the pleasure of hearing such a voice, though I've heard many accounts of it in others' visions."

Osmond and Inara peered at the man through furrowed brows and squinted eyes.

"I understand your suspicion. I've seen it before."

The older gentleman stood beside Osmond's booth and bowed before the three.

"Allow me…I feel as though I'm past due for introducing myself. My name is Geronymau, an old defect of the Mounean Order. I'm quite sure any tales I recite will likely leave you even more dazed than you are now."

Geronymau's smile seemed to ease into the crevices of his cracked cheeks, emanating a vibe of eeriness complied with a slight comfortability.

"Thank you, this food looks impressive!"

Osmond slid his oversized plate closer to his chest and inhaled a massive whiff of the dish.

After shifting her slice of cheesecake to the right of the table, Inara returned her focus to the small, greyed gentleman to her left.

"So, you understand the significance of this voice in Osmond's dreams?"

"More than you'd imagine. More than I'd like to know."

"What is this Infinite Operator and how is it attached to the Mounean Order?"

Geronymau's eyes sparkled at the sound of the question, revealing all the signs of an overdue anticipation longing to be fulfilled. It wasn't until he saw Andres staring at a spot outside on the street that Geronymau realized the odd grouping he had met.

"Not the most attentive when uninterested," Geronymau sighed.

"It's been a while since I've discussed the order…yet you three are now as closest to Kipinntak without being in it. I suppose you'll have to be a little knowledgeable about its origins if you're to be in the area."

Osmond slid towards the wall, so the senior could sit down.

"You might be able to fend off the cult's advances, but their teachings lend attractive reasoning. My time built around them gave me a unique perspective towards the group. You look at me with a doubt and slight perplexity, I presume. Let me persuade you of my words' validity."

"Well, y'know… How does a generous guy like you get wrapped up in a group like the Mounean Order? Those people can be so… hardcore."

"*Ha hah,*" yes, all valid points. Believe it or not, I've been a part of the order since I was a child. I was born in Kipinntak, the birthplace of the movement. Although they absolutely can be *hardcore*, I never let their actions misguide me from the initial message."

"Well, actions tend to have a louder voice than words. That had to be one hell-of-a message," Osmond said between bites of his breakfast.

"That it is, my friend. It is mainly holding the collective dear, so no one is left behind."

"Sounds a bit like the cogs should be concerned with the welfare of the wheel. The results you're looking for are found when everyone takes care of their self. It makes for a much smoother ride."

"Yes, of course! That's an argument often made to counter the order's base philosophy. Excuse me, dear," Geronymau said, looking at Inara.

"You haven't touched your cheesecake at all. Trust me, it's one of their best items on the menu!"

"I believe you, I'm just not in the mood for it anymore. I had a well-sized lunch."

"In that case, do you mind?" Geronymau asked with grateful eyes.

"Thank you, you're too kind, my dear. All three of you are wonderful. Ever since I left the order, I haven't had the opportunity to converse with others from outside this area. This is nice," he said.

The doorbell chimed as two widely-draped figures in white staggered in from the dusty sidewalk out front. Both bulky and unkind to the ground they cracked.

"Wah-tor, madam!" one immediately beckoned as the other diverted to the restroom.

His voice was as heavy as the coat shrouding his entire physique.

The giant white shadow flung his hood back revealing a shiny pale orb. He stretched his neck, cracking bones that moved like iron.

Besides his large size and cold skin, the bald visitor might have appeared like any other in the diner, if not for the metallic lobes that chronicled the circumference of his head.

"Speak their name and they shall appear," Osmond whispered, facing down at his clean plate.

"We're just in luck. Who better to learn about the order than someone who currently follows it?"

Geronymau moved closer to the edge of his seat until his arm was swiftly grabbed by a delicate, yet firm grip.

Inara stared into Geronymau's eyes and said, "Thank you, Geronymau, but that won't be necessary. You've already told us more than enough of what we need to know, and we've finished eating, which means our time is up here."

"Oh… well, I understand. It's certainly been a pleasure chatting with you all. Truly!"

"No, no. Just the wah-tor. Dat is it!"

The rumbling sound of the man in the white coat vibrated across the diner to Osmond's side successfully ending his prior conversation.

As the second man in a white coat returned from the restroom, he flipped back his giant hood, revealing two metallic patches. One spanning over his jaw to his clavicle, and the other squarely on his left temple.

His line of sight leveled with Osmond's table and even more so with the inventor's eyes. He stared until he sat down on the stool beside his partner who quietly sipped water from his paper cup.

"Sven, are you done? We need to get back."

The heavy-voiced man sipping his free drink appeared to ignore the man sitting beside him loudly demanding action.

The words, "Leave dem alone," rang through the floor of the diner, ending the conversation between the two.

"Phor, trrr-ust the process," Sven said loud enough for all of Osmond's table to hear.

As the tall pale figure stood up from his stool he was met by the diner's most genial, old gentleman.

"Phor, Sven… I remember when you two were shorter than me!" Geronymau chuckled lightheartedly.

"Wha… Do we know you?" Phor questioned.

"Of course, it hasn't been that long since I had a white one like yours."

"*You* were a part of the order?" Sven scoffed.

"You're de size of my youngest daughter."

The Mounean men seemed to have a hardy laugh at the feeble ex-member.

"Yes," Geronymau sat on the stool beside the two, "I am a bit petite, but that never held me back from fulfilling plenty of missions. Wawae Islands, Pragnanz, Tanahabu, even ultra-covert tasks in Orion's Eye. You don't know of the history you mock. You see these lines," Geronymau pointed to his face.

"They aren't laugh lines. They're quite the double-edged faults."

Phor and Sven jeered at the random old man until Phor froze, mouth agape. He had noticed the table from before was now absent of its other three members.

Phor tapped on Sven's arm and pointed to the empty booth.

Sven's harsh grimace grew into a smirk as he slid off the stool.

"Clever old man, you probably were covert in all those places."

Sven then turned to his friend and shouted, "Never mind him, let's move!"

Before the two could take one step from their seats, an identification card was placed between their faces.

"How about now? You rascals still think I'm some fictitious storyteller?!" Geronymau proudly shouted.

"Huh… Geronymau Ituly, Searcher. I see… Okay, old man. I believe you," Sven muttered under his breath.

"Now, we need to go follow those three you ate with; the Order depends on it," Phor shouted.

"Well, no need to be rude."

"Sorry, old man, but it's getting late," Phor said, shoving Geronymau aside.

"If you understand at all what we're scouting, you know we need to follow them. You know the choice for the whole is never left to one," Sven stated.

"Why are you following those nice people? What could they have possibly done?"

"Look mister… Ituly. If you were a member of the Mounean Order, den you realize we take orders from the highest."

"Yes, the Infinite Operator," Geronymau said quietly.

"Exactly… den you know we must go," he slowly articulated.

"De Infinite Operator commands it!" Phor shouted.

Sven bent down and locked eyes with the senior who stood at his chest. While bent over, his voice rumbled in the back of his throat with the ferocity of a grizzly bear.

Neither fear nor panic flowed through Geronymau as the giant brute lingered over his face.

With an assumed satisfaction, both turned away from the short old man and headed for the exit.

Sven was stopped short by a ring from his pants pocket.

As he reached for his phone, the lobes protruding from his bare head flickered with a dull white glow.

"Who is it?" Phor asked.

"Probably Madam. Hello?"

Sven and Phor flipped their hoods atop their heads as they pushed through the diner doors.

The day had blackened and shadowed the diner. Few lights on the street compared to the night ahead.

Left standing, staring through the swinging doors at the two giant men on their hunt was Geronymau. He knew what they were in search of had only existed before in rumors, but he never could have expected to meet it in his lifetime. He considered himself lucky to have met the fabled Infinite Operator.

XXIII. Silent March

A red light overhead flashed green as Andres advanced through the light rail's security gate.

Andres, Inara, and Osmond paced through the rails' doorway and passed all the passengers until they arrived at the back of the cart.

Hanging from the ceiling, separating every five rows were small dimly lit signs that read "**LIMAR VALLEY**" in a dull green light.

Once the air brakes squealed, all the passengers comfortably leaned back in their seats and faced forward with their hands on their knees.

The train's force barreled each person deeper into their cotton comforters without fair warning.

Andres looked up just as the letters on the Limar Valley sign broke down with pixilation, readjusting into "**CAB.**"

The sign's green glow blended smoothly with the bright silverfish aura emanating from the night sky.

A cool, peaceful mood situated in Osmond even with his particular circumstance, as the grisaille pastiche painting his window navigated him to a calmer place. Underneath his folded arms and face, hidden in the glass was a slight smirk with barely risen cheek bones.

Osmond had the entire two-person seat to himself, though he tried not to over extend.

In Inara and Andres's row, shade was cast over both seats from the moon's silvery ray.

After several minutes of hearing the train's engine and harsh current created by the rail, Osmond grew used to the sounds of the speeding carriers and naturally toned the rail out as a deep hum.

While remaining still and facing forward, Inara and Andres's eyes homed in on movement over a dozen rows down the cart.

Glued to his window, Osmond carefully observed the red distant mountains outlining his view. The further the light headed east, the smaller the mountain range shrunk.

Limar Valley's red sands proved ever-increasingly dissimilar to the fertile soil covering all Libe Villages, of which was the firm foundation for Osmond's upbringing.

In a swift, hurried motion, Osmond shifted his neck towards the aisle and rotated his legs to the wall of the carriage. His singular movement helped his sight down the rows of seats and allowed him to better hear the light footsteps approaching the back of the cart.

To his surprise, the muffled taps on the floor spawned from a tall, lean man in a dusty beige coat.

The long figure glared behind him at the others sitting in the back, effectively chilling the air in the whole back portion of the cart.

Once Osmond stared the tall, gangly passenger up and down, he slid back into his seat, returning to his slouched position.

Careful not to look away, Inara watched the tall, new passenger adjust in his seat. None of his movements surpassed her observation. His breathing appeared stable and heavy, complimentary of his stature.

Inara started to rise above her seat until she was stopped at a moment's notice.

Andres's arm was stretched before her waist, preventing her from standing up.

Unsurprising to him, Inara frowned out of frustration, perplexed why her counterpart was holding her back from the inevitable confrontation.

Andres returned the puzzled look with his usual stoic expression and placed his index finger perpendicular to his lips.

He pointed at Osmond who was fixated on his window, eyes halfway open.

Looking at Inara, Andres signaled behind them pointing backwards then he pointed at three spots ahead of their seat.

Inara fell back to her seat as her surge of unease transformed to helplessness.

Adding to her discomfort, Andres continued signaling to the select points from before, this time tapping his ear.

After she peeked at the spots Andres pointed at, Inara sighed then turned to Andres, who was once again focusing on the people across the train.

Her raised eyebrows and widened eyes almost slipped passed Andres that she was curious as to what next to do.

Andres faced forward to avoid any unwanted eyes and simply bounced his hovering hand down signaling to Inara.

Inara raised her thumb in approval and sat back in silence.

Osmond had curled up in his open booth quietly resting, while Andres and Inara observed the seats around them and constantly split their focus across the train.

Hours passed for all the passengers, of whom were mostly asleep, except for a couple in the back that remained vigilant and concentrated their focus on the other passengers the entire way.

A screech was forced from beneath the rail and all movement halted across every row in the cart.

Osmond sprung to attention as a voice from above announced their arrival.

"Hello passengers and welcome to Cab, the megacity over sand!" the intercom announced.

"Well, back to our town of escape," Osmond jokingly said.

Inara glanced at Andres who gave a short nod of approval. She then grabbed Osmond's hand and rushed to the front of the train cart. Andres lingered behind at a sluggish, yet attentive pace.

The three hurried before any other passengers took to the aisle, leaving everyone else to fumble luggage in mass amongst themselves.

Few were left to exit once Inara and Osmond stepped off the train, thus several rows of heads held still staring straight ahead.

Before Andres took his last step on the light rail, five people across the train all stood at once.

The five scurried to the doors in a desperate rush, all while keeping quiet.

Their drab coattails flapping in the wind were the only sounds heard as they moved through the rail station.

"Relax, Inara," Osmond shouted. "We're far enough into Aryeh that I'm sure no one has taken notice of our whereabouts."

Inara quickly glared back at Andres as soon as Osmond finished giving his reason for comfort.

Her disheveled expression aptly explained to Andres her unease with their current situation, though Andres closed his eyes and shook his head in disapproval.

Clasping Osmond's hand again, Inara jerked him forward saying, "Come, show us where you friend lives. The night has arrived and will only grow at this point!"

"Fine, sheesh!" Osmond said, feeling rushed. "Two blocks south and we're there. What's the sudden urgency? Is it because of that tall man on the light rail? I'm sure he's gone by now," he said, checking behind him.

Andres slowed down behind the two even further, careful not to alarm any suspicion.

The crowd of people bunched behind Andres moved slowly along the sidewalk, though he watched to be assured they showed no signs of strange behavior.

Osmond directed his excited friend through the dusty streets leading out the city's nucleus and into his old neighborhood.

"Who knows… Benoit might be glad to see Andre and I return since last time our meeting ended rather abruptly."

"You're referring to your time fleeing Orion's Eye to eventually staying with Sofia?" Inara coyly asked.

Osmond quieted, was unsure how to answer. He felt responsible for intertwining his friends in something he initially started as an experiment. Guilt plagued him to no end, though he continued his path.

"Oh, come now. I meant that as a joke. I don't want you to be down about Sofia," Inara said.

"It's... fine. I want to make sure Benoit is not put in the same line of fire as we've gotten ourselves into. Whether the Mounean Order chooses to follow the peaceful option or force," he said pointing at Inara's stomach, "shouldn't be of any concern to Benoit's life. I would hope he has been living quietly since I returned to Chun, and if so, I'd like to keep it that way."

"No need to worry. If we're as close as you say we are, we should be able to stay and regroup until morning. Once in front of a computer I can attempt to track the movements of Iri and her followers, and better escape to someplace. At least until the 4DM warms up."

Trying to refrain from reacting, Osmond briefly glanced at Iri with a puzzled look.

"Okay, that sounds good, I guess," Osmond said. "Just ahead, those tall street lamps light the entrance of the neighborhood. Andres, I'm assuming you remember the way from our last trip here...right?"

"Yes," a soft but stern voice stated from behind.

Osmond immediately looked back to understand the difference in tone but found only a young man gazing ahead with serious intent.

"Okay, well... this is the block," he said still peering back at Andres with one eye.

As the three approached a stoned fence, Osmond halted at the gate of the wall's anterior then reached in his front pocket to grab his phone.

"Hello... are you there?"

"Osmond, where are you right now?!" the phone screamed.

"I'm standing outside Benoit's front gate with Andres and Inara."

"Well, I had some people from VIDE track the Kipinntak Prime Minister and they've returned with results."

"What are you trying to say, she's in town? Spit it out, Ehmen," he said in a frustrating tone.

"No, I'm saying she's at your friend's house now! Get away from that property immediately!"

Osmond looked at the surrounding sidewalks at the two standing beside him. A stern reflection of his younger self stared back at him in a disapproving manner, while a young woman, of comparable age, held a blurry-eyed gaze at the ground beneath Osmond.

"Hey, Ehmen... I'm gonna have to call you back."

"Ozzie, are you leaving?! Ozzie... answer me!" the phone's speakers pleaded before Osmond silenced it by hiding it back in his pocket.

"He's right," Inara softly spoke, "we should leave now."

"But what about Benoit?" Osmond asked.

"Earlier you said you couldn't explain why, but we need to visit Benoit. Is this why?"

Andres, completely quiet until now, walked closer to Osmond.

"I couldn't explain why before, yet knew we needed to come here. Though my vision has grown exceedingly clearer, I still cannot provide you with the answers you seek."

"Ugh," Osmond sighed, "but you're saying we should still go inside, right?"

Only a glance at Osmond was returned from the rhetorical question, although he felt an answer in the stare.

He begrudgingly walked passed the stone gate and up the front steps to Benoit's door.

Before now, opening this entrance typically meant no knocking or any semblance of notification. Osmond saw this house as his shelter for three years while living with Benoit.

A small light above the door illuminated Osmond's hand on the doorknob, reminding him how dark the night had become, reigniting a sense of urgency.

As the door crept open, a light voice called from the living room shadowed in a sable blanket.

"Osmond? Oh... you came. Um, I was hoping you wouldn't this time."

A lamp near the front door slowly sparked to a yellow flame, flooding the entire room.

"Benoit," Andres said.

Osmond's eyes adjusted to the room up to his eventual confirmation that it was his friend leaning forward on the couch before them all.

He began to step closer until stopped by Andres's arm stretched in front of his chest.

"Finally, we meet," a voice said from beyond the dark hallway.

The three standing at the lit door were now completely aware of the trap prepared at their expense.

"Prime Minister Iri… what is this?" Osmond asked.

Moments after he finished speaking, the door behind the three budged against Inara's back, pushing her into Osmond and Andres.

In a swift sequence of movements, Osmond stumbled forward, and Andres held the flung door still, while two large men in robes slipped through the cracked entrance.

"Rrright on time, I see," one muttered aloud to the other.

Once Osmond peeked back, he immediately recognized the giant figures in white.

"Ah…well, that explains those two. I'm assuming they've been following us since we left Orion's Eye. Alright, go ahead and tell me…what do you want from Andres and I?"

"Want?" the voice asked from the hallway's void.

A distant clicking on the hardwood floor echoed from the darkness until a meagerly tall, pale woman emerged from the abyss. Her long, dark red braid swung with energy and a commanding force she was renowned for across the regions.

The small square-framed glasses sitting low on her nose reflected the lamp's soft glow, completely clouding any sight the others had of her eyes.

"You actually believe we *want* something from Andres or you?" she asked.

"We do not let personal impulses dictate our actions. You have been misguided on our group's functions."

She sat on the couch beside Benoit, who was fidgeting and tapping his foot.

Osmond looked over his shoulder at the two men hulking over Inara and Andres.

"If that's the case, why go through all the trouble to gather us? You can't possibly think we'd accept a friendly conversation as the reason," Osmond said.

He saw Iri's eyebrow instantly raise above the brim of her glasses.

"No harm intended. You certainly seem very loquacious, just not too friendly," Osmond continued.

"Osmond!" Inara responded. "This definitely isn't the time to hurl insults at the Prime Minister."

"Oh… so you *are* familiar with who I am! You can be quite rude, Dr. Diaz. But this one…" Iri said standing up.

She approached Inara, coming within centimeters of her face.

"You don't get nervous, do you?" Iri asked. "That explains so much. How else could someone be as equally gorgeous and symmetrical as the gods themselves. You, my darling, are honestly the finest work of art I've ever seen."

Iri leered at Osmond from the corner of her eyes and said, "The one redeeming quality about you."

"Art should always be revered when recognized, no matter who the artist may be," she said holding Inara's cheek.

"Alright," Osmond shouted, pulling Iri's hand from Inara. "Enough focusing on her. She's none of your business!"

From the dark crevices of the hallway, stairs, and kitchen appeared several large men in white robes. Their hooded coats shone a foggy grey while intersecting the shadows and the room's weak light.

"None of my business? I believe we're at odds if you truly believe that statement, my dear."

"Then explain, why have you been following us the past few days?!" Osmond exclaimed.

"A mutual benefit, Dr. Diaz. My concerns aren't mine alone. I'm simply attempting to preserve all of Juk in all its prosperity."

Iri's crimson braid swung from shoulder to shoulder as she yanked her hand from the confused man beside her and turned around.

At the cue of her movement, the looming figures in the shadows appeared at her side.

"Calm down, I'm fine," she said to the lurking robes in the darkness. "Not that you need to know the details of my business, but I'm on a mission. As technology advances beyond our wildest dreams, so should the composition of us. I started the Mounean Order with the hope of connecting all people, emotionally, physically, and psychically. With a world of intersecting minds, so much strife and misuse could be avoided. The possibilities abound all limits."

"Of course, I seem to be hearing that a lot lately. But what does that have to do with Andres?" Osmond asked.

"I'm sure you know the answer to that question, Dr. Diaz," Iri said as she returned to the couch Benoit was now leaning back in.

While Iri's back was turned Andres gave a lightning-quick glance to Inara, who responded immediately by rummaging one hand through her bag.

Eyes forward and remaining still, Inara dug through the bag for a few seconds before removing her hand.

As Iri sat down, she said, "You created one of the world's most integrative and expansive artificial intelligence systems, possibly ever seen by any human to date. I'm sure you're aware of its capabilities, whether favorable to humanity…or not. It should be of no surprise I contacted the beneficiary of such an impactful device."

"If you wanted help on developing a communication system, why not ask?" he angrily asked.

"As I stated before, Dr. Diaz, I have a mutual benefit with others. Many others. You created one of the most advanced intelligences this world has known."

Iri stared at Andres then asked, "Did you think you could ever contain such a brilliance? Something that shines brighter than your imagination could possibly conceive. I bet Andres here has performed countless tasks that you might not have ever considered. Life isn't his prerogative; command lines are his priority. He has one objective in mind and that's to conclude his current task. Ask him, is humanity of any concern to an android sophisticated as himself."

From his peripheral vision, Osmond peeked at Andres, which remained still behind him until now.

Andres stepped in front of Osmond and Inara, returning Iri's glare with a cold, stoic stare of his own. In the dimly lit room, his brown eyes appeared as frozen wax.

"If I go with you, what would happen to Osmond and all the others?" Andres questioned.

"Truly living up to be a model of your creator, and not just on looks," Iri responded. "No need to ask a question of which you know the answer. There would be no reason to bother Dr. Diaz or his friends if you joined the Mounean Order's work and complied with our requests."

"What if I simply left? Osmond could help you create an advanced communicative network, but I would remove myself from all of society. Inara as well," Andres said.

The hypothetical question caught the attention of all in the room, causing everyone to fixate on the android.

"What you propose sounds great but, how would you accomplish something like *that*?" Iri asked.

Andres grabbed Inara's hand and walked to the center of the room.

"I assume you're being truthful. If not, this decision can easily be reversed."

A high-pitched screech pulsated from the center of the room, causing everyone present to hold their ears in extreme caution.

Since the immediate reaction to the shriek was covering his ears, Osmond hunched over looking down at his feet.

A white light creeped towards Osmond feet, which were now shaking with the entirety of the house. The white energy overtook the lamp's modest ember and painted every corner of the living room and hallway.

As briskly as the light and pitch materialized, their absence occurred even quicker, leaving all in a relatively dark and now quiet salon.

"What was that?!" Iri shouted.

Osmond's eyes lingered on the floor of the room's center until he readjusted to the dim light. A slight smile seeped onto his face as he rubbed his eyes.

"Where did he go?! They're both gone! What happened?" Iri screamed at Osmond.

"Where, I couldn't tell you. As far as when, I'm sure it's a long time from now," he said smirking.

Now, in a room filled with strangers, only the sound of panting lungs was heard.

XXIV. In Absentia

A padded exhale rushed from the door locks of the compact jet as four placid creatures calmly stood at the exit.

In front was a moderately tall woman with dark amber hair that fell neatly to her shoulders. The shimmering brown curls were identical to the hazel orbs staring down towards her feet.

At each leg of the noticeable beauty was a small child with similar features.

The woman and her two children inched near the cliffside's edge, fully observant of the vast city buried underneath in fog and smoke.

"Look, Mama, clouds!" one of the young boys shouted, pointing in the distance.

"Yes, Ovid. They are certainly interesting, aren't they?!" a firm, statuesque man said as he descended from the ship.

"The stoic figure had a full black beard tinged with gray streaks thinner than silk webbing on a branch.

Though his attire was typical of a middle-aged man, the faint wrinkles on his face barely revealed his years.

If not for his greyed strands and washed-out clothes, he would have easily been mistaken for one that was newly experiencing maturity.

"Not quite what it used to be, huh?" the man asked the slightly younger woman now bending over with the children.

"It's so drab and gray, it's clear the Mounean Order's involvement has loomed over this city for an extended era. In the many years I stayed here, I'd never seen as much smog as this dusty blanket covering my city. There's no green in sight!" she replied.

"A shame, no?" he said while closing the jet's door.

He held the back of both boys' heads as he stared at the cityscape.

"You see that massive white tower far out passed the water? That's Orion's Eye Observatory. Your grandpa's friend used to run that place."

"What is that place, Papa?" one of the boys asked.

"That, my son, is where some of the world's most renowned astrophysicists worked."

"And so much more," the woman said, turning around. "That island is where curious minds observe this universe's giant structures and activities. Idle minds tend to wonder loosely at that place. Well… they did when I was last here. It has been so long since we've been here, I'm sure no one we once interacted with still remains."

"You might be right… If so, we shall see soon," he said, pacing to the forest's entrance.

"Come, this is the quickest way to the city."

The young boys looked up at their mother with wide, uncertain eyes.

"Are we going down *there*?"

"Yes, Orpheus… we are. Don't worry, it'll be fine. I doubt it's as scary up close as it is from this mountainside.

Libe Villages always embraces its guests with a warm welcome. You'll like it," she assured the nervous boys.

"Yeah, and if it doesn't prove itself to be as hospitable as expected, Orion's Eye is only a train ride away."

She sighed and said, "Don't act that way…" nodding towards the children below her.

"You'll spread that negativity, if not careful, Andres."

He laughed and replied, "You're probably right. Let's go."

The heavy fog, thickened by pollution, suddenly brightened to an unclear canary as the small family trekked through the woods to Libe Villages and the sun returned to its shift.

"Here it is in all its glory, Libe Villages Park!" the father announced to his family.

"Um… not the greatest reveal," the mother replied.

"Andres, let's hurry passed this area. It doesn't seem…" she whispered while fixated on the people in hooded robes passing by, "… too welcoming."

Of the dozen people passing by, five were cloaked in anthracite robes from head to ankles. The remaining few were dressed in typical garbs Andres had expected: dull shirts and dark pants, reminiscent of his old friend's wardrobe.

While focusing on those walking by, Andres noticed a trend among them. Each had a distinct glimmer around their neck or eyes.

"Inara… these people."

"Yes, I see. We should head to the observatory. You two want to see this world's *biggest* telescope?"

Both boys cheered for the device, though their jubilee was mostly fueled by their eagerness to evacuate the sullen park.

"We can use the Chariot to get there quickest. Ugh, this place is nothing but a graveyard surrounded by cracked statues and rusted benches. Not at all what I envisioned."

"It's fine, dear. There's still more to explore," Inara said.

Immediately, she grabbed her son's hands and retraced their steps through the park entrance to the steep cliffside.

Andres opened the ship's door to a wealth of security guards that were all prepared for a litany of reactions.

"Sorry, all. We didn't mean to disturb anyone, we're simply here to speak with Dr. Kriit," Andres pleaded with the guards.

The security detail promptly paused, then looked at each other in confusion.

"Didn't realize that was a weird question," Andres muttered as he turned his head.

Though murmured, he overheard a guard whisper to another that the ship must be interfering with their eye scanners.

"Could one of you assist us with finding Dr. Kriit?" Andres asked.

"Which Kriit are you wanting to see?" a guard asked.

Andres stared at the person asking the question and began processing the situation.

"Inara, Dr. Kriit had two children, correct?"

"Yes, Robert and Isaac. Both should be well-aged with families of their own by now."

"I see. Well, I assume they're both in control of the facilities. Could we see whichever one is near?"

"Let me get in touch with Isaac Kriit and see what he thinks. He might be in his office," a guard said while holding up his wristwatch.

A few guards huddled up while the one communicated with his watch.

Inara walked towards the ship's entrance with their sons close behind.

"Maybe it was a mistake coming here… and now," she whispered to Andres.

"No, this is the time. I'm sure of it. We just need to speak to one of these Kriit brothers and figure out where he is."

"Okay, sir. Mr. Isaac is open to speaking with you in his office. He sounds excited to meet you all, so let's head there now."

"Sounds good to me. Come on, Inara… boys."

Andres and Inara's family followed the guard to the telescope's base and into Glen's former office.

A large bearded man stood at the hallway's base as Andres first opened the door. His silhouette would have easily covered the entire door frame.

"Hello, you wanted to speak with me?" the massive figure bellowed.

His voice echoed throughout the hallway, not unlike Glen Kriit.

"Yes, my name is Andres, this is Inara, and our two sons, Ovid and Orpheus. We knew your father many, many years ago and wanted to visit…for memory's sake."

"You don't say?! Now that I see you up close, I recognize *you*. I met this gorgeous lady when I was first beginning my university studies," Isaac said, rushing towards the entrance.

"Miss Brillar, how have you been?!" he asked, reaching to hug Inara.

Isaac's reach consumed her entire body simply with his forearms.

Inara could not help but smile as the burly lumberjack lifted her with both arms wrapped around her back.

"Father would be so happy to see you here again! What brings you into town?"

"Well, we're having a bit of a vacation while on Andres's business trip," she said.

"Really?" Isaac said before stepping back and looking at Andres.

"Excuse my absent-mindedness. Call me Isaac. It's nice to meet you."

Andres shook the offered hand hovering in front of him.

"Don't worry about it," Andres quickly replied.

"And you're Ovid, correct? You have fascinating eyes, Ovid. They're almost ethereal, like small self-aware pools. How old are you, big guy?"

"I'm five years old!" he shouted at the kneeling giant.

"*HAH HA HAH* Perfect! What about you, young man? How old are you?"

"I'm eight."

"Hmm, you sound like the big, strong brother. Do you look out for this guy?"

"Yes!" Orpheus instantly replied.

"Isaac! I hate to rush to the point, but I'm curious of where I could find someone. Osmond Diaz…Where has he gone?" Andres asked.

"You want to see Dr. Diaz?"

The liveliness in Isaac's eyes drained into his limbs as he nervously fidgeted.

"From the look on your face, I'd say Dr. Diaz is no longer around," Inara said. "No worries, we assumed as much. You seem like you've seen a ghost," she laughed.

"I…just figured you knew since Andres is Dr. Diaz's son," Isaac said.

Inara briefly peered at her companion who mirrored her expression.

"Oh yes, of course I know," Inara responded after looking at Andres.

"So, your father *has* mentioned me," Andres asked.

"Yes, definitely. He said he met you once in person but spoke with you many times over distanced communication. He deeply and earnestly valued your talks, which I'm guessing were discussed over the phone. Since you were looking for my father, have you seen Ehmen?" Isaac asked.

"No, I didn't expect him to be around. Where is he now?"

"Where do you think?" Isaac asked with a glimmer in his eye. "He still works at the massive VIDE, Inc, constantly developing new products and streamlining old ideas."

Inara turned to Andres and said, "Ehmen must be nearly 90 years old by now. We should stop by VIDE to see him."

"Yes," Andres said before hushing and glancing at Isaac.

"Oh, no… Don't feel obliged to stay here with me. It's been so long since you've been in Chun. Please, go see Ehmen for me. He'll surely be ecstatic. And tell him I said 'hi' since he never comes to this side of the eye anymore," he said.

At the doorway near the family, Isaac stood nearly twice as tall as the couple before him and roughly five times the height of the young boys. Yet still, Ovid and Orpheus looked up to the sky-high statue with endearing grins.

"Thanks, Isaac. It was great seeing you. It's almost as if I was talking to Glen again," Andres said, holding the door open.

Inara and her boys crept out of the hallway onto their next stop, while Isaac continued talking with Andres, who stood in the doorway.

"Not a problem at all! It's such a surprise seeing you in person. My father always referenced how brilliant and amazing Dr. Diaz's son was, though I was never able to place a face to the description. I've got to say, I'm jealous! It'd mean a lot to my brother and I if you'd visit again for a longer stay," Isaac eagerly rambled.

"Of course, we're on a schedule this time, but I look forward to meeting Robert as well."

"Oh, Robert will be so jealous!" Isaac said grinning ear-to-ear.

"We all kind of expected your return; after all, Dr. Diaz assured we'd be seeing you someday. We just weren't sure how long it would be. Nonetheless, I'm glad you returned."

Andres suddenly paused after walking through the door then glanced back at the giant figure filling the doorway.

"Osmond awaited our arrival?" he asked.

"Ha, you're surprised?" Isaac joked closing the door behind Andres.

DING

The elevator bell rang as they reached the 55th floor and the overhead lights dimmed.

The moment the sliding doors cracked open, Andres rushed through as if late for a meeting, while Inara dragged behind holding their two sons' hands.

"It's strange seeing this place look as similar as it did all those years ago," Inara said.

The three behind Andres focused on the metal cavern within the building's center glass wall.

Within the cylindrical glass wall, which stretched from the top to an indiscernible basement floor was a plethora of balconies. Each had a group of people in lab coats meticulously inspecting some device.

Ovid and Orpheus looked in pure wonder, while Inara deeply glanced through the clear walls with skeptically heightened brows.

"I hope we're catching him at a decent time," Inara said, still staring through the wall.

Andres firmly knocked on the office door, careful not to shake the door too vigorously.

"Hello, Ehmen. It's Andres and Inara."

Within seconds, several locks between the door and its frame could be heard shifting to one side as the large metal slab pushed open.

"Oh my! The old fool was right," a tall shriveled man said, slightly hunched over.

Inara's eyes twinkled as she moved in front of Andres and cheerily said, "Surprise!"

Her exuberance mustered a faint grin on the aged portrait of her old associate.

"Unbelievable...I can't believe it. I suppose where you've been all these years is the real question," Ehmen said before his deflated chest forced him to pause. "But I'd love to know why you've returned."

"Over fifty years later and you still sprint to the point," Inara said to the spindly, greyed engineer.

His laughter was fragmented between chuckles and coarse coughs, prompting him to take a seat near his desk.

"You realize the confliction that comes with living a full life? You see the birth of many humble beginnings grow into great wonders worthy of gratitude...and sometimes endless admiration," he said looking at Andres.

"You see such immaculate, artistic structures, physical and conceptual. And you get a first-hand show of those very structures' downfall."

He stopped to cough for a few seconds, hacking into his hand and lap while instinctively concealing his feebleness.

Inara compassionately observed the embattled engineer as Andres, Ovid, and Orpheus stood silently behind her.

"You probably don't remember the last time I came here, do you?" Inara asked.

"Don't count me out just yet," Ehmen replied, "but refresh my memory a bit."

"Our meeting proceeded your talk with the Prime Minister of Kipinntak. It wasn't exactly a war of words as much as it was a volley of threats," Inara reminded him.

"Yes!" Ehmen said, clearing his throat.

"I'd never forget that day. The workings of that day changed *everything*. Since you two have been gone, influence from the Kipinntak government has exponentially grown. Chun has strengthened the relationship with our neighboring regions, Kipinntak and Aryeh."

He stopped to inhale, then continued.

"The world is a far different place than when you left it. We can't always be lucky enough to escape our fates like ole Osmond," Ehmen said, winded.

"Actually, that brings us to another point. What happened to Osmond? According to Isaac Kriit, Osmond let it be known he believed we would return to Chun," Andres stated.

"Oh, yes… yes. You wouldn't believe how he went on about you. You'd have thought he expected a son away at war to finally return," Ehmen joked.

"Hmm, yes…" Ehmen looked at the four in his doorway, completely in tune with every movement of he made.

"Come," he said leading them outside his office and to the elevator.

"Wait, Ehmen! Where are you going?" Inara asked.

"You… asked where he was at. I'll show you exactly where to look. But first, how did you get here? These old bones have become accustomed to personal car seats. I'm not sure I could take a light rail in this condition. Proper posture is no longer a leisure I can ignore, but rather a standard I long to regain."

"In that case, you'll be glad about our recent mode of transportation," Andres said, closing the thick VIDE door.

"Here, land it here!" Ehmen's tired voice strained.

"Sir, why have we come to Libe Villages park? We stopped here earlier and weren't impressed," Inara said.

Ehmen turned to Inara and softly said, "I told you I'd take you to him. We may not have had a healthy relationship towards the end, but he was once a young brother to me."

"All this talk of the end, you'll depress yourself," Andres said guiding the Chariot to a dead patch of grass.

"Here's a good spot," Ehmen said as he rose from his seat.

Before everyone could exit the aircraft, Ovid and Orpheus stood on their toes at the window and peered at the familiar wasteland.

"Hey, we were just here," Orpheus exclaimed. "Why are we back?"

"I almost forgot to mention. Inara… you had children?!" Ehmen asked with tightly pursed lips. "That's amazing! I couldn't imagine a better mother. And Andres here is their father, I'm assuming?"

"Yes," Andres simply stated.

"Well, I guess it's never too late to learn something new," Ehmen said under his breath.

As Ehmen exited the Chariot, he waved his arm in front of him as if he was wafting an ill scent.

"I can see why you all had such a quick stop here before. From the looming fog and dead trees to the suspicious characters walking about, this isn't a welcoming place anymore. Certainly not what you think of when park comes to mind."

After examining Andres, Ehmen reasoned the blank expression was indicative of agitation, an estimation that would have normally been spot on.

"Understood," Ehmen said. "You see that lonely plot near the crooked tree? There's our guy."

Andres wistfully stepped over to the short tombstone inscribed "Osmond Andre Diaz" and held a placid gaze until the others approached from behind.

Inara brought her two boys next to her and kneeled at the stone slab.

She gracefully removed her golden link necklace and placed it on top of the tombstone, allowing the circular pendant to dangle at the front.

Inara's action forced a partial smirk on Andres's unchanging face, thus he took off the golden chain hiding underneath his shirt and placed it atop her necklace.

Since the pendant was a vertical bar, its intersection with the first golden pendant created perfect symmetry, a clearly intended act from Ehmen's perspective.

"It was in Cab while he was visiting Benoit," Ehmen blurted during the silent stares at the grave.

"I'm sorry?" Inara questioned.

"Osmond. He died some years ago while vising Benoit. The cause, I'm not too sure on. According to Benoit, he faded during his sleep. Not quite the calamity as anyone who knew Osmond would have expected, but it's how I'd like it to happen. I'd rather time have its way than the exploits of man."

Ehmen ran his bony finger across the top of the tombstone and said, "Only a few days after the incident, his casket was shipped back to Libe Villages where he lies now. An extremely expedient process, minus any fanfare."

Steeply focused on the plot before him, Andres did not react to Ehmen's statement, unlike Inara who held her hands together in front of her chest, brooding at the details.

She appeared to be lost in thought until a shrug on her coat pocket made her privy to the young boy pointing at the tombstone.

"What does that mean, Mama?" Ovid asked.

Inara followed the child's finger to a quote under Osmond's name.

The quote read:

"Anyone can provide an adequate answer; true importance lies in finding purpose for the question. Now, what do you want?"

"I was never solidified on that line's meaning, but we can be assured it's not something he would have taken lightly. In fact, Benoit stressed this was inscribed on his tombstone, more so than any other accommodation," Ehmen said.

A brief distinct chuckle arose from Andres while he turned towards the Chariot.

"Well, he did accomplish what he wanted. Come, Ehmen, we'll take you home," Inara said grabbing her boys' hands and following Andres to the aircraft.

"Thank you, dear. It has been a treat spending time with you all," Ehmen cheerfully said.

"It always is," she replied.

Andres glanced back at the hunched-back legend of his time and said, "Don't think of this as another ending. This is only the beginning."

About the Author

James Tyler Copeland is an emerging American author from the Charlotte metropolitan area. He was born in Bethesda, Maryland, though he spent most of his time in North Carolina, where he studied for an undergrad philosophy and political science degree. Throughout his time at UNC-Charlotte, Tyler always managed to discuss life's unanswered questions and values, thus he spent frequent time with the university philosophy club. His science-fiction (SF) writing was heavily influenced by the late SF authority, Isaac Asimov, as well as the legendary SF tale by Mary Shelley, *Frankenstein*. With *Flawed Machines*, he hopes to reach an understanding of purpose that has often gone overlooked.